MYSTERY OF THE NIGHT RAIDERS

ALSO BY NANCY GARDEN

THE FOURS CROSSING BOOKS

Fours Crossing

Watersmeet

The Door Between

What Happened in Marston

Berlin: City Split in Two

The Loners

Vampires

Werewolves

Witches

Devils and Demons

The Kids' Code and Cipher Book

Annie on My Mind

Prisoner of Vampires

Peace, O River

MYSTERY
of the

NIGHT
RAIDERS

MONSTER HUNTERS
CASE #1

Nancy Garden

FARRAR · STRAUS · GIROUX
NEW YORK

With special thanks to Betty Johnston, V.M.D.,
for medical information about cattle and bats. Any errors
that remain in these areas are mine, not hers.

And with thanks also to Richard A. Greene, D.M.D.,
for advice about how to make the teeth.

For the Blakes:

David, Irene, and Wayne,

and especially for

my fellow mystery, fantasy, and horror fan,

Adam

CONTENTS

MYSTERY OF THE NIGHT RAIDERS

ARRIVAL

"WHITE RIVER! White River Junction!"

The Vermont Trails bus lurched as its air brakes hissed, and Brian Larrabee was thrown sharply forward in his seat. Rescuing his book, *The Collected Sherlock Holmes*, with one hand and the smaller of his two suitcases with the other, he murmured, "Excuse me, my stop," to the elderly lady sitting next to him, and climbed over her into the aisle.

Only a few other people got out in the small Vermont town. Brian himself was headed south, to his grandparents' farm near the village of Grove Hill—a long way from the noise and excitement of his home in New York City, which he'd left early that morning.

A long way in more ways than one, Brian mused as he waited outside the bus for the driver to fish his other bag from the jumble in the bus's luggage compartment. Not that he didn't like Vermont; he loved it, and had visited the farm nearly every August of his thirteen years. But this summer was different. The Paragon Theater, two blocks away from the apartment Brian shared with his parents and his little sister, Joanna, was having a Sherlock Holmes film festival, and Brian knew his visit to Vermont was going to cost him at least four adventures with his favorite sleuth.

"Bri! Hey, over here, son!"

Brian turned to see his grandfather, a tall, slender man whose white hair had once been as black as his own unruly thatch, leaping from his dilapidated pickup truck and waving frantically.

"Hi, Grandpop!" Brian shouted, feeling his face break into a grin despite his mixed feelings about being there. "Be right over." He spotted his battered tan suitcase wobbling plumply on the sidewalk where the driver had just set it down, grabbed it, and ran to his grandfather's truck.

Grandpop seized the larger suitcase and gave Brian a squeeze with his free arm. "Well, aren't you a sight for sore eyes," he said, beaming. "You sure do cheer a body up. Hop in. Dang truck's been starting sluggish lately, and she'll stall out in a minute if we don't get started."

Brian chuckled. Grandpop had had the truck, Old Blue, for as long as he could remember, and she'd never been any more reliable than she seemed to be right now.

"How've you been?" asked his grandfather, after

heaving Brian's suitcase into the back of the truck with the energy of a man half his age. He held the tailgate open till Brian had thrown in his smaller case.

"Still reading Holmes, I see," remarked Grandpop, slamming the tailgate shut and fastening it with a bit of wire.

"Sure am." Brian went around to the passenger side and climbed onto the high seat, holding the book on his lap. "There's something new each time." He'd started reading Sir Arthur Conan Doyle's stories about the great English detective two years earlier when he'd been recovering from an emergency appendix operation, and he hadn't stopped since.

"Well," said Grandpop, easing in the clutch and accelerating with a series of machine-gun-like backfires, "I sure wish I had someone like Holmes around the farm these days."

"How come?" asked Brian.

"Dang cows're sick."

"Oh." Was that all? Mildly disappointed, Brian shifted his gaze to the window, where the familiar white houses soon gave way to equally familiar round hills and mountains.

"Trouble is," said his grandfather, accelerating more to pass a crawling car, "no one can figure out what's wrong. Not the vet, not the county agent, not anyone."

Brian turned back, his interest kindled now. "How come?"

"How come! I don't know how come. It's no disease they know of and they just can't figure it out, is all. Seen nothing like it, they say. And they're right about that." Grandpop turned gloomily onto the highway. "I've been farming fifty years, and I've never seen anything like it either. But I've already lost four good milkers." He banged his hand on the steering wheel as if to dismiss the thought. "Enough of that. You're a city boy, not a farmer. How're your folks? How's that swim team shaping up?"

For the rest of the trip they talked about family and about the YMCA swim team Brian had finally made after a year of hard training with his coach at school. The team had won meet after meet during the early part of the summer, and Brian had proved himself to be one of its most valuable members. That was another reason, of course, why he'd been reluctant to leave the city.

He was just telling Grandpop about a big meet during which someone from another team had tried to kick him underwater, when Grandpop turned Old Blue down a narrow dirt road lined with apple trees on one side and a couple of cow pastures on the other. A small black and white dog sprang from behind an especially gnarled tree and threw himself furiously at the truck's right front wheel. "Dang beast," said Grandpop good-naturedly, screeching to a stop and reaching across Brian to open the passenger door.

Brian barely had time to put his book down before

the dog leaped onto his lap: Brian snuggled his face into the long, barn-smelling hair. Cadge was more than just a pet border collie and one of Brian's best friends; he was also Grandpop's main farmhand. "My cowboy," Grandpop often called him, saying, "There's no better herder anywhere in New England."

Right now, Cadge was covering Brian's face with ecstatic sweeps of his slippery pink tongue and seemed anything but the professional he was. But Brian knew that was the way of border collies: intense about everything—work, play, and friendship.

A few minutes later, Grandpop pulled Old Blue up to a rambling white farmhouse. Brian jumped out, and a short, plump woman with a rose-colored dress just showing around the edges of a huge white apron ran down the broad porch steps to greet him. Brian had always been a little embarrassed by Grandmom's enthusiastic greetings. But when she'd come to New York to help nurse him after his operation, she'd spent day after day bringing him snacks as well as his regular meals, and she'd talked the doctor into letting him swim a week earlier than the usual post-operative schedule said he should. He was hardly going to begrudge her the usual enveloping hug. In fact, he hugged her back, hard.

Afterward, she held him away from her at arms' length. "My, you're getting to be a handsome one," she said admiringly. "Still that slender swimmer's build, still that tangle of hair." She brushed it back off his forehead. "Still that strong jaw and those snapping black eyes." She clucked her tongue. "Brian, Brian," she said, "it won't be long before we'll have trouble keeping the girls away from you."

"Now, Jessie," said Grandpop, handing Brian one of his suitcases and his book. "Don't embarrass the boy, for pity's sake. Didn't you say something about giving us lunch when we got here? It's nearly two."

"Lunch it is," said Grandmom, releasing Brian at last. As they went up the steps with Cadge bounding joyfully in front of them, she added in a softer voice to Grandpop, "Sam, the county agent called again. He wants the vet to run some more blood tests on the cows. And that Mr. Greerson from the milk co-op wants to drop by sometime soon and have a talk with you."

When the screen door closed behind them, Brian heard the unmistakable sound of a bellowing calf. He turned, and seized his grandfather's arm in alarm.

A Holstein heifer calf, with the beautiful black and white markings of her breed, had just staggered up to the near pasture fence—and collapsed in a quivering heap on the ground.

NUMBLES AND DARCY

"CALL THE VET!" Grandpop shouted, tearing across the driveway and through the gate leading into the near pasture. Brian followed with Cadge.

The calf was trembling and seemed barely alive; her eyes were dull and her breath was coming in slow shudders.

Grandpop bent over her. "It's like the others, only worse. Poor little mite; it's as if she's too small to take whatever's wrong." He passed his hand gently over the small body, whether feeling for something or trying to comfort the animal or both, Brian couldn't tell. "Funny thing is," Grandpop said, straightening up, "she was right as rain at ten o'clock last night. The others've sickened slowly before they died—'course, they've all been full-grown cows. But I didn't even notice anything off about this 'un. Can't say as I looked too close today, though." He ruffled Brian's hair. "I was in a hurry to meet someone at the bus."

"Grandpop," said Brian, who'd been thinking hard all this time, trying to apply Holmesian logic to a situation that seemed to defy it, "could she have been poisoned?"

His grandfather gave him a blank stare.

"Well," said Brian, half apologetically, but in earnest, too, "I was trying to figure out what would make an animal seem sick when it didn't have any disease anyone knew about, like you said. Couldn't poison do that?"

"Could." Grandpop walked over to Cadge and gave him a pat; the dog was huddled anxiously a few yards away. "But how in tarnation would she get hold of poison?"

"I meant could someone be trying to poison your cows," said Brian patiently. "Deliberately. That would explain how she got it."

Grandpop looked thoughtful. "It's an interesting theory, son," he said finally, kneeling beside the calf again. "Especially since my herd's the only one around here getting sick. Trouble is, I can't think who'd do a thing like that. Far as I know, I haven't got any enemies. Still . . ." He put his fingers into the calf's mouth, forcing it open, and then leaned down, sniffing.

"Cyanide smells like almonds, I think," said Brian. "Or is it arsenic?" Holmes would know, he thought irritably. I'd better brush up on my poisons!

"I don't smell anything I shouldn't smell." Grandpop sat back on his heels. "Sorry, son."

"Mind if I look around a bit anyway?"

"Nope. Go right ahead. You can do anything you like this first day. Just remember to be back in time for supper. And that chores start tomorrow."

Brian nodded. He'd always helped out on the farm, and had planned to make a special point of it this summer. "Grandpop may seem strong," Brian's father had said in New York before Brian had left that morning. "But remember he's seventy-eight. You make sure to do your share of work around the place."

"I'll be back soon," Brian said to Grandpop. "Can I take Cadge?"

"He's got chores himself." But Grandpop's face soon softened. "Well, okay. Just today. He deserves an afternoon off."

"Thanks, Grandpop," Brian said, and turned to go, but was stopped by the sight of his grandmother, apron flapping, running toward them, something in her hand. "Vet's on his way," she panted when she reached them. Then she thrust a small package at each of them. "You never did get your lunch," she said. "Figured now you'd be staying with the calf. How is she?"

"Alive," said Grandpop, looking sadly down at the motionless black and white heap. "But weaker'n a newborn." He held up his sandwich. "Thank you, Jessie," he said. "Brian, you marry a woman half as good as your grandmother and you'll be getting a prize."

"Oh, bosh," said Grandmom. But she looked pleased nonetheless.

Brian stuffed his sandwich into his pocket and whistled to Cadge, who trotted along beside him willingly as he turned out onto the driveway and headed toward the dirt road that led into the main one. He'll have come by car, Brian guessed; the poisoner.

But the weather had obviously been dry for some time, and it was impossible to isolate tire tracks in the loose dust of the road.

"Of course he wouldn't *have* to have come by car," Brian said to Cadge, who was sniffing around an old stump. They were now walking along the far pasture fence; one end of the far pasture wrapped around the near pasture, separated from it by a dirt path, like the bottom part of a huge L. "A car would've been noisy. Maybe he came on foot."

Cadge waved his scuffy black and white tail, and cocked his head.

Brian knelt in front of him. "Could you track him? Has someone been here, boy? H'mm?"

But Cadge either didn't understand or didn't choose to; he just wagged his tail.

Brian looked out across the far pasture. Grandpop's farm was in a wide, flat valley between two sets of mountains, a little like a Western canyon, but not as steep or closed in. There was only one road through the valley, though there were several across it leading into the mountains. Brian realized all the dirt roads would be equally dry and dusty; footprints would be as hard to pick out as tire tracks, if not harder. And nothing would show on the paved road. I'll have to think of another approach, he decided; Holmes would.

A person intent on one thing might be careless about others. Wouldn't Holmes look for something the poisoner had dropped, or a hole he'd forgotten to close up in the fence?

The fence! That was it! Whoever it was would have had to crawl through its barbed wire, or toss the poison over it. And he'd probably have had to put it in some kind of food—grain, or hay, maybe, or salt; didn't cows like salt?

Brian ran back to the path between the pastures, Cadge close behind him. It would be boring to examine every inch of wire, but that's what Holmes would do.

Cadge bounded ahead, but Brian walked slowly, his eyes riveted on the fence and on the ground beneath it, looking for a scrap of fabric torn off the poisoner's clothes, a bent or broken wire, even a chunk of salt lick . . .

"Watch it!"

Brian pulled up, and realized he'd nearly walked smack into a plump red-haired boy who was squatting on the ground at the edge of the path, holding Cadge away with some difficulty.

Brian's heart raced. The poisoner? Returned to the scene of the crime?

But Cadge seemed to know the boy, and the boy

certainly knew Cadge, for he was addressing him by name and telling him to mind where he put his paws. "You, too, please," he commanded Brian amiably.

"What—why?" asked Brian.

"Because I've just found a snake nest and if you step on it you'll squash it even more than it's been squashed already."

Snakes! Could that be it? Could a snake have done it? Or . . . " 'The Adventure of the Speckled Band'!" Brian exclaimed. "That's it!"

"Conan Doyle," said the boy promptly. "*Will* you get out of the way?" He didn't sound quite so amiable this time.

"Sorry." Brian stepped back. "It's just that my grandfather's cows have this strange illness and I wondered if someone's been poisoning them, and when you said snakes, I . . ."

"You thought of 'The Adventure of the Speckled Band,' in which Sherlock Holmes finds that the murderer is using what he calls a swamp adder as the murder weapon. The guy trained it to obey a whistle, didn't he?"

"Yes," said Brian, excited all over again now, for he'd never found another person his age who had the slightest interest in Holmes. "He put it through a ventilator, where it had no place to go except down a bell rope right onto a bed that was clamped to the floor. He'd trained the snake to come back when he whistled, and he'd already killed one of his stepdaughters that way, and was going to kill the other, when Holmes took the case. I'm Brian Larrabee," he added.

"Obviously," said the boy. "Mr. Larrabee's grandson."

Brian started, then realized that he'd already mentioned his grandfather's cows and that the boy knew Cadge. And of course Grove Hill was so small that pretty much everyone knew everyone else's business; it wouldn't take much to figure out who a stranger was.

"The snake killed the murderer in the end, didn't it?" the boy said. "My name's Edward, by the way. Edward Crane."

"Ha!" came a scornful voice from somewhere above them.

Brian looked up and saw a small wiry girl about his age, wearing rumpled green shorts and a smudged blue T-shirt. She was perched on a branch over both their heads.

"Edward Crane, *Junior*," announced the girl, jumping down and landing between them. "But that's his fancy name. Most everyone calls him Numbles."

Brian suppressed an involuntary laugh; the boy, looking disgusted, turned back to the rock he'd been squatting beside.

"His little brother couldn't say 'mumbles,'" explained the girl. "So when their parents were talking one day and said 'Edward mumbles,' he thought it was part of Edward's name, only he said 'numbles' instead. It stuck."

"Too bad nothing like that ever stuck to you," Numbles retorted, carefully moving the rock aside and scraping at what looked like a pile of old sticks. "Let me introduce you, Larrabee. This is Darcy Dixie"— here he dodged a swat from the girl—"Verona, who unfortunately lives down the street from me in the village, and who fortunately goes away to school most of the year. Luckily we only have three more weeks to go before we're rid of her till Thanksgiving vacation."

"Hi, Darcy Dixie Verona," said Brian, liking her in spite of Numbles's introduction. She didn't seem silly or giggly like most of the girls he knew.

"I won't use Larrabee," Darcy said shrewdly, "if you won't use Dixie. Deal?" She stuck out her hand.

Brian took it. "Deal."

"Don't you like Larrabee?" asked Numbles mildly, putting on a glove and pulling something carefully out of the small indentation in the ground where the sticks and the rock had been.

Cadge watched with great interest.

"Not a lot," Brian admitted.

"Too bad. Sounds very high class." Numbles examined what he'd removed from among the sticks. "Blast it! They're all dead."

"All what?" Brian asked, squatting beside him.

"His stupid baby snakes," said Darcy. "Numbles is

· 16 ·

crazy about reptiles. Anything that crawls, wiggles, has little pop eyes, cold blood, and looks like it ought to have slimy skin even if it doesn't. Yuck."

"They're *black* snakes," Numbles informed them. "Black racers, to be exact. *Coluber constrictor constrictor*, at least I'm pretty sure that's the proper name. You see, Larrabee—er, I mean Brian—they can't be your speckled band because they're not poisonous. In fact, there aren't any poisonous snakes around here except . . ."

"One just moved," interrupted Darcy, who by this time was squatting opposite the boys, peering at the dead snakelets. She looked fascinated, not at all like someone whose reaction to reptiles was really "yuck."

"What?" Numbles bent closer.

Darcy pointed. "That little one. It twitched its tail."

Carefully, while Brian edged in to see, Numbles lifted the thin wormy-looking reddish-blotched bodies away from each other one by one, eventually exposing one that wiggled slightly; it was tiny and weak, but definitely alive. Its little tongue flicked in and out of its mouth when Numbles touched it.

"Good eye, Darcy," Numbles said dispassionately, carefully picking up the snake and holding it away from Cadge's inquisitive nose. "I'd have missed it." He stood up.

"Now," said Darcy, "he's going to take the squirmy thing home and give it its own house, and sit up with it for hours like some kind of nurse. Bor-ring!"

"Want to come, Brian?" Numbles asked, ignoring Darcy and popping the snake into a sturdy muslin bag. He pulled his glove off and stuffed it into his pocket. "We could continue our discussion of the speckled band and your grandfather's cows."

"Sure," said Brian eagerly. "Come on, Cadge."

"You know, I've got a theory about that," said Darcy, falling into step beside them. "Mr. Larrabee's cows, I mean."

TEX AND COMPANY

IT WAS "The Adventure of the Speckled Band" and other Holmes stories, not Darcy's theory, that dominated the conversation on the way to Numbles's house in the village. When they got there, Numbles led them to the back of the house, and asked that Brian leave Cadge on a small screened porch. Then he took them through the porch and inside to a large glassed-in room.

"Wow!" exclaimed Brian, looking around at the cages and tanks that lined the walls, while Darcy perched on a stool near a table piled high with books and papers. "This is something!"

Numbles smiled in obvious satisfaction. "Yes, it's not a bad collection for a beginner," he said. "Let me show you around. This"—he indicated a small-mesh wire cage—"is Tex. He's a Texas horned lizard—*Phrynosoma cornutum.*" He pointed to a placard affixed to the side of the cage. "Most people call him a horned toad, but he's not a toad at all."

"Isn't he hideous?" said Darcy, hopping off the stool and peering over Brian's shoulder at a squat brownish creature with a snub nose and two short horns at the top of its head—rather like a miniature foreshortened dragon, Brian thought. Its back was covered with shorter horns, and it blinked as they stared at it.

"My uncle sent him to me," said Numbles, opening his muslin bag and carefully releasing his new baby black racer into a small aquarium, empty except for sand, sticks, and bits of bark on the bottom. He took a saucer from the table, filled it with water from a tiny hose, and placed it in the sand on the bottom of the aquarium. Then he turned back to Tex's cage, and sprinkled the plants that grew there. "Most lizards can't drink out of dishes the way snakes can," he explained. "But they can lap up drops. They don't last long in cold climates, either, so I'll probably send Tex back to my uncle for the winter. My uncle's a herpetologist. He lives out West and has horned lizards practically all over his back yard."

"A what?" asked Brian. "Your uncle's a what?"

"Herpetologist. Person who studies herps—reptiles. That's what I'm going to be, too. Why don't you go ahead and look around while I make out a tag for this guy?" Numbles gestured toward the baby snake and then took a white index card off the table.

"Here, look at this one," said Darcy. "It's my favorite." She stopped in front of another aquarium, this one with water in it.

"Favorite!" snorted Numbles. "Don't tell me you actually like one, Darcy! Which?"

"The dog one." Darcy nodded toward a foot-long creature swimming in circles. Its blunt nose and rounded forehead did indeed make it look dog-like, as did its lightly spotted body, which stretched out like a dachshund's, complete with tiny legs. But, unlike a dachshund, it had a huge bulbous tail, just about as wide as its body. What struck Brian most, though, were the maroon plumes that waved gracefully from behind its head, like a circus headdress, a little in back of where one would normally expect ears to be.

"This is Fritz," said Numbles. "He's a mudpuppy." *Necturus maculosus*, Brian read on the label. "That fancy hat he's wearing is really his gills; he gets oxygen through it. My grandmother brought him from her pond in upper New York State; I've been observing him all summer—see?" He flipped open a small file box and displayed a pack of index cards closely covered with meticulously neat notes. "I'll be sending him back, too, at the end of the summer."

"Do you always let things go?" asked Brian.

"Usually. That's what a good herpetologist does. Why keep something in captivity unless you have good reason to? Tex is a pet, though; my uncle will return him to me if I send him back for the winter. And I've got a snapping turtle out back I've had since I was nine. I'm sort of trying to tame her. Want to see? Then we can get to work on the problem with your grandfather's cows."

"Sure," said Brian.

"Later you can come over to my house and see my softball trophies," said Darcy in an undertone as they released Cadge and went down the back steps into a small yard. "Do you play any sports?"

"I swim," Brian told her, leaning down to pat Cadge, who was jumping on him joyfully. "No, Cadge."

"Yeah?" said Darcy. "Well, all right! So do I! I got to the top group in Scout camp real quick when I went, and I'd swim more here if it weren't for softball, which I like better. Team sports are more fun, you know? Except I kind of like running; do you run any? He's hopeless as an athlete," Darcy said, jutting her chin out toward Numbles, who was beckoning them over to a fenced-in enclosure whose wire walls leaned inward.

Brian took a firm grip on Cadge's collar and looked inside. The enclosure was dominated by a pool made of stones set in concrete, with several large stumps and bits of branch strewn on the ground around it. A lean-to shelter with a few bushes nearby filled one end, and at the other, glowering at them malevolently, was the ugliest creature Brian had ever seen — much uglier, to his way of thinking, than Tex. Its head was large and heavy in proportion to the rest of it, and its tail looked like a thick upside-down saw, teeth pointing up.

Cadge barked loudly.

Darcy laughed, but Numbles looked alarmed, so Brian led Cadge to a picnic table at the other end of the yard, and said "Down!" and then "Stay!" firmly.

Cadge looked unhappy, but he was too well trained not to obey.

When Brian went back to the enclosure, Numbles was climbing over the fence, with half a head of lettuce in his hand. "Hi, Rosey," he called cheerfully. "How you doing, girl?"

The ungainly creature bobbed her head up and down a couple of times and lumbered up to Numbles, taking the lettuce from him as gently and delicately as a kitten might.

"Wow," said Brian. "I thought a snapper would bite a person's hand off."

"Most would." Numbles climbed out again. "And she'd probably bite anyone's but mine. Rosey and I know each other pretty well. I'm trying to show," he said solemnly, "that even the most hostile of creatures can be tamed. Of course reptiles aren't long on brains, but I'm working on that, too — you know, trying to develop what little intelligence she has. I have a pretty big file on Rosey." He reached toward a shelf attached to the fence, on which, under a little roof, stood four file boxes — but Darcy yanked at his sleeve impatiently. "Oh, come on, Numbles, that's enough of your slimies for one day. We've got to figure out about those cows. And I'm starved. Have you got any food?"

It was then that Brian remembered his sandwich,

which he discovered was two instead of one—slightly mashed baloney and cheese, but perfectly edible. Numbles disappeared inside his house and brought out some Cokes and cookies, and the three of them sat around the picnic table, Cadge at Brian's feet, munching in contented silence for several minutes.

"Now," said Numbles, wiping his mouth and throwing a bit of crust to Cadge, who caught it deftly, "about your grandfather's cows. I really don't think it's a snake, because poisonous ones are so rare around here. Of course there *is* the timber rattlesnake, *Crotalus horridus horridus*—"

Darcy snickered, and Numbles glared at her.

"—but we're a little outside its usual range," he went on. "Reptiles do stray sometimes, but it seems pretty unlikely; my dad says there hasn't been a timber rattler here since he was a kid. Besides, I don't think they're poisonous enough to kill cows, and I also don't see why they'd keep going back to them. A rattler wouldn't want to eat a cow, so it'd only bite one if it was scared, and it wouldn't go back to the same place to be scared again." He took a swallow of Coke. "It's amazing how little people know about snakes. Even Conan Doyle. I've tried ever since I first read that story to figure out what he meant by a swamp adder."

"The most poisonous snake in India, he says," Brian told him.

"Right," Numbles answered. "I know he says that, but as near as I can find out, there's no such thing.

Of course, common names are always a big problem. They change from place to place, which is why I use Latin names whenever I can. No, the closest I can come to that swamp adder is Russell's viper—*Vipera russelli*. It's very poisonous and from the right area, and it's sometimes called an adder—that's not a very scientific name, by the way. But . . ."

Darcy gave a tremendous and very loud yawn. "Borring!" she said, swinging her legs impatiently under the table. "Doesn't anyone want to hear my idea before I have to go to softball practice?"

"I do," said Brian, remembering she'd said something about a theory when they'd been on their way over. "What is it?"

"That it's not a snake poisoning your grandfather's cattle." She lowered her voice and looked around dramatically. "That it's a person!"

"Oh, come on, Darcy," began Numbles, but Brian stopped him.

"I thought that, too," he said, "until I started looking around. So far I haven't been able to find any evidence for it, though. And no motive either."

"But the idea makes sense," said Darcy, standing up and stretching, then bending over and touching her toes. "Sheesh, I'm stiff. Too much sitting." She waved her arms in circles. "Hey, you're the Sherlock Holmes nut, Brian, right? Evidence is your job." She joggled Numbles's shoulder. "Remember you promised to come to the game tomorrow. Or rather, you promised Jeremy you'd take him. Jeremy," she said to Brian, "is his little brother. The one who gave him his nickname. Now, *he's* an athlete. See ya!" With a final swing of her arm, she ran off.

"She pitches," said Numbles, looking after her. "So does Jeremy. They both like basketball, too. It's a beautiful friendship, I suppose. But as she says, bor-ring." He reached for a cookie. "Look, Larrabee — er, Brian. I suppose she's right about her theory, evidence or no evidence. It does seem like the only thing left, if the vet rules out disease."

"I know. I think that's what Holmes would say, too."

For a moment they sat there in silence, while Cadge and Rosey stared at each other suspiciously across the yard.

"We could," said Numbles tentatively, "try finding out about poisons." He drained the last of his Coke. "I don't mind looking things up," he said casually.

Brian figured he was telling the truth, given all those card files. "Great!" he said excitedly. "That'd be terrific. We could make a study of poisons, 'a small study,' as Holmes would say."

"*And* convince the vet to do an autopsy," said Numbles. "That'd help, too."

"Don't you think he'll have done that already?"

"Well, you can find out, can't you?"

The autopsy idea turned out to be a dead end. The vet had done several, Brian learned at dinner that night.

"He didn't find anything," said Grandpop, passing the gravy to his wife. "Not a thing. Just the usual scratches and insect bites, and a little anemia. Low blood volume, he said, but with no sign of internal bleeding. A mystery."

"Yes, but was he looking specifically for poison?" Brian asked suspiciously.

"What a terrible thought!" Grandmom ladled gravy over her mashed potatoes and passed the gravy dish to Brian. "I can't think of anyone who would want to do that. Not any more, certainly."

"What on earth do you mean 'not any more'?" asked Grandpop.

"Oh, there was that trouble with George Knowles."

"Ha!" Grandpop exclaimed scornfully. "That's what I thought you meant. But he wouldn't have had the gumption."

"Who's George Knowles?" asked Brian.

"An old farmhand of mine." Grandpop cut a drumstick off the roast chicken and plunked it onto Brian's plate. "I hired him last fall to help out around the place. He seemed like an educated fellow, maybe a bit too much for a farmhand, but he needed the job."

"Softhearted," said Grandmom, "that's what it was. Your grandfather felt sorry for him."

"Yes, well, I might have saved my feelings," said Grandpop. "Knowles turned out to be a lazy son-of-a-gun, and I had to fire him."

"Grandpop," asked Brian eagerly, "couldn't that be a motive?"

"It could." Grandpop helped himself to grape jelly. "If he were still around. But he died late last spring."

"Oh," said Brian, disappointed. He slipped a little chicken to Cadge, who'd been lying hopefully at his feet. "Well, could there be anyone else?"

"No. I told you before, no one. Brian, like I said, it's a good theory. But I'm afraid it just won't hold up."

"Unless it's some maniac," said Grandmom thoughtfully. "Some crazy person."

"Right," said Brian, seizing on that idea. "So wouldn't it be a good idea to ask the vet about poisons anyway? I mean, it wouldn't hurt, would it?"

"I already did," Grandpop said gruffly, "just this afternoon." Then he added. "See, I'm not so dead set against your idea after all. When I asked him, though, he said no. No sign of poison at all, not even snake venom or poisonous plants. It's something to do with the blood, like I said; maybe a parasite. The county agent's testing the water now, from every stream and brook and pond on the place. Catching insects, too, and testing them. And checking grass samples for parasite eggs. I don't think it's a poison, son, not even a natural one."

But Brian wasn't so sure. He thought about it all evening, and was barely able to concentrate on the

TV program he watched with his grandparents in the large comfortable living room. He was still thinking about it when he said good night and went upstairs with Cadge, who trotted along beside him and curled up with a sigh at the foot of his bed when he climbed in.

For a long time Brian lay awake, watching the progress of the stars across the sky and trying to think of all the Holmes stories with poison in them. Didn't Holmes say someplace that some poisons are hard to trace, he wondered. Or impossible? Or did I read that somewhere else? No matter, he decided—if it's true, the vet wouldn't have found anything even if he'd looked for poisons when he did his autopsies.

But how does one trace a traceless poison?

As Holmes would say, he thought sleepily as he dropped off, fully a three-pipe problem. If only I were old enough to smoke!

A THREE-PIPE PROBLEM

CHORES BEGAN IN EARNEST the next morning, so Brian didn't have much chance even to think about poisons, except briefly when Grandpop told him the calf had died during the night and the vet had already taken her body away. Then in the afternoon there was Darcy's softball game; she telephoned him at lunchtime and reminded him of it, so he felt he had to go.

Brian had expected only a few parents as fans, but was surprised to find the rough wooden stands so crowded he had to squeeze in beside Numbles, who was sitting next to an eager-looking skinny kid of about nine.

"Hi," said the kid, leaning across Numbles's plump body and smiling stickily around a red Popsicle. "I guess you're Brian. Hey, is someone really poisoning your grandfather's cows?"

"And I guess you're Jeremy," said Brian, remembering what Darcy had said his name was. "I don't know about the poisoning. But I'm going to try to find out." He turned quickly to Numbles; the players were already taking their positions. "The vet says there's no sign of snake venom, or any other poison. But I've been wondering about traceless poisons—if we could find out about them."

"Batter up!" called the umpire.

"The library," Numbles shouted in Brian's ear above the roar that accompanied the home team's first pitch. "We can go right after the game."

"Aren't you guys going to watch?" asked Jeremy disgustedly, poking his brother. "We're going to wipe the Foxes out. Our team's the Wolves," he said to Brian—and Brian turned his attention to the field. Holmes, after all, used to go to concerts to clear his mind when he was on a case. Besides, it was only going to be a seven-inning game.

It was very nearly a no-hitter for the Wolves, Darcy's team. She started pitching in the fourth inning, struck out everyone easily, and did the same in the fifth. Her arm and body worked in one motion, smooth as a swimmer's, Brian had to admit, and the ball flew with deadly accuracy, right at the edge of the strike zone. "She's got a terrific eye," whispered Numbles begrudgingly in the sixth when she'd struck out the Foxes' two star batters for the third time; the score was 4–0 Wolves, with only a little more than an inning and a half to go. "It's true; she can spot a newt a mile away. Sometimes I have to take her with me when—oh, no!"

Brian heard the crack of bat hitting ball, and a roar went up from the Foxes. Seconds later, Darcy swiveled toward first, her face set and angry. The ball had skimmed straight at her along the ground, fast and hard, but she'd managed to stop it and now she hurled it at the first baseman—and the runner leaped triumphantly onto the bag a split second before the ball arrived.

"Safe!" yelled the umpire, and Jeremy groaned.

"It's good for her," said Numbles, taking a squashed chocolate bar out of his pocket and dividing it into thirds. "No-hitters go to her head."

Something seemed to have snapped in Darcy, and she walked the next two batters, which meant there was a runner on each base.

The coach ambled out to the mound.

"Oh, no," said Numbles. "If he takes her out, there'll be no living with her for days. Please don't take her out, don't take her out, don't . . ."

He didn't take her out.

When the game started again, the Foxes booed and hissed and yelled and clapped in rhythm from their bench, but Darcy stood firmly on the mound, her eyes steely and her jaw set.

"Look at her," said Jeremy. "Just look at her! Not even Roger Clemens looks like that. Go, Darce!" he yelled. "You can do it!"

"Shut up," said Numbles. "Don't rattle her."

"She can't be rattled," said Jeremy. "That's the great part. When she looks like that, she doesn't hear anything or see anything except the batter; she told me. Total concentration, she calls it."

There was a sudden hush as Darcy cradled the ball in her hands—and a groan when she stepped off the mound and scratched her head, pushing her cap askew.

"On purpose," whispered Jeremy. "Tensing up the batter. Oh, she's using all her tricks now. She's got it; she's hot now."

"Can't you shut up?" Numbles unwrapped another chocolate bar and poked it at him. "Here, stuff your face, alien."

"Yuck," said Jeremy, pushing it away. "How can you think of food at a time like this? Creep."

Brian didn't say anything; his eyes were riveted on Darcy. "Total concentration" was one of the things he admired in Holmes, too. If she could apply that kind of effort to something non-athletic—looking for evidence, say . . .

"Streeeeike!" yelled the umpire. The Foxes' groan was drowned out by the Wolves' cheer—but Darcy's face remained impassive.

"I bet she doesn't even sweat when she's like this," whispered Numbles, wiping his brow.

"Streeeeike!" yelled the umpire again.

Darcy turned around to face the fans, and grinned

toward where Brian, Numbles, and Jeremy were sitting.

"She doesn't even know she does that," said Jeremy. "I told her about it once, and she said she didn't remember. It's a reflex, sort of. Total concentration."

"Oh, sure," said Numbles. "More like total show-off."

Darcy's arm went back again, and the ball shot forward, fast and slightly curved.

The batter swung . . .

. . . and missed—and the Wolves burst onto the field, surrounding Darcy, hugging her, slapping her shoulders.

"There's another inning and a half," someone shouted. "For Pete's sake, cut it out!"

But the Foxes had fallen apart. They allowed two runs when the Wolves were up in the last of the sixth, and when they came up in the seventh, they swung at anything Darcy pitched, and went down one, two, three.

The crowd went berserk. Jeremy grabbed Brian's hand and tugged him toward the Wolves' bench, yelling, "Come on!" Numbles followed at a more dignified pace.

It took them a couple of minutes to work their way through the mob around Darcy; she elbowed her way to them. "Hey," she said to Brian, after hugging Jeremy and slapping Numbles on the back, "you saw it, huh?"

"Pretty good, Darce," said Numbles coolly, "for a girl."

"Oh, come on, you jerk," said Jeremy. "Good for anyone, you mean."

"It's okay, sport," said Darcy affectionately. "I'm used to it." She turned to Brian. "Enjoy the game?"

"Yeah," he said. "Yeah, I sure did. You were—terrific."

"Not so terrific there in the sixth," she said, sobering. "Sheesh, I thought I'd die when Coach came out to the mound. I had to do some fast talking after that second walk."

"It was total concentration that did it, huh, Darce?" asked Jeremy excitedly, jumping up and down.

"Yeah, kid, I guess so. Why? Did I have that look?"

"Oh, yeah," said Jeremy. "Man, did you have that look!"

Darcy grinned, and then glanced back at Brian. "Too bad it's so close to the end of the season," she said. "We could have used another first baseman."

"I'm all thumbs with a ball," Brian said. "Really."

"No one's that bad," Darcy said generously. "Anyway, we've still got to swim together. I bet you could beat me in a race. Crawl?"

"Anything," Brian said.

"How about now?"

"Well . . ."

"He might have better things to do," said Numbles. "Like—" He looked expectantly at Brian. "Like a certain bit of research."

"You could paddle around while we race, Numb," said Darcy. "Or look for minnows or something. Hey, Brian, how about it? I could run home and change real quick. Of course I guess you'd have to go all the way back to the farm . . ."

"Thanks anyway," said Brian. "How about tomorrow? Numbles is right. We were planning to go to the library."

Darcy made a face at Jeremy, who grinned.

"To look up about poisons," Brian added hastily. "Traceless ones."

Darcy brightened. "Hold on," she said. "Let me go home and change and I'll meet you there. It's only a block away. Traceless poisons, wow!"

"She sure is something," said Brian, watching her go.

"Yeah," said Numbles, "but what? The trouble with her is she's all action and no thought. You know what I mean?" He gave Jeremy a little shove. "You were going to Donny's after the game, remember?"

"Maybe. What's a traceless poison?"

"One no one can find any sign of in a dead body. Hey, go on, you were going to shoot baskets or something. Let's see how fast you can run."

"Oh, come on, Numbles, I'm not a little kid any more." Then he fell back in mock horror as Numbles lunged at him threateningly. "I'm going, I'm going. See you around, Brian!"

"Yeah," Brian called after him. "See you! He doesn't seem so bad," he said to Numbles.

"All little brothers are bad. You got any?"

"Sister," said Brian. "She's a pest sometimes. Other times, I don't know. She can be okay. And once when she was sick I got real worried."

"Yeah, I know. Happened to me once, too. But still, he's like Darcy, all action. Should have been her brother."

They were walking off the field now, and soon they turned down the village's short main street, which was lined with large leafy trees, maples, most of them, and white houses.

"Does Darcy have any brothers or sisters?" Brian asked curiously.

"Nope. I guess that's why her folks can afford to ship her off to that fancy school down south—Maryland, I think it is. They've got horses there, and the kids're supposed to learn how to be ladies—it's all girls." He laughed. "I can't blame her parents for trying, but I think it's pretty safe to say that nothing's ever going to turn Darcy into a lady. You'd think they'd know it by now, too." He turned up a curving cement path that led to a low red stone building with an arched front door. "Some adults are kind of slow to catch on, I guess. Here we are." He opened the door, and Brian, following him inside, was immediately struck by the smell—cool and a little stale, as if last winter's air had somehow been trapped inside.

Now for the three-pipe problem, he thought.

"Why don't I take the card catalogue?" Numbles whispered, obviously feeling right at home. "I'll just write down anything that looks possible, and then get the books off the shelves. You could start with the encyclopedia." He pointed to the far corner, where Brian could see the spines of *Collier's*, the *Britannica*, *World Book*, and one or two others lined up neatly on the shelves.

A young-looking librarian with long blond hair smiled at them as they passed; Brian was relieved to see she didn't seem the type to shush people.

For the next forty minutes or so, Brian pored over encyclopedia indexes and articles. Numbles joined him then with a pile of books, saying, "I think they don't dare have books on poisons. There are a few on plants that include poisonous ones, and I've got them here, but there aren't any books just on poisons themselves, let alone any mention of traceless ones."

"Probably," said a loud female voice, "because they don't want people doing in their grandmothers. No offense, Brian."

He looked up to see Darcy in a fresh pair of shorts and a clean T-shirt, her hair damp and curly, bending over the table and scanning what they were reading. "Sheesh," she said. "That's grim. 'Kills by convulsions and suffocation.'"

"Grim," said Brian, closing the book, "but no good. Grandpop told me most of the cows just sort of faded away. Nothing dramatic, except with that calf I told you about."

"Chronic poisoning," said Numbles, looking up from the volume in front of him. "That'd work for the fading away. When the victim gets small doses over a period of time."

"Yeah, well, look at this." Darcy eased down into a chair and read aloud from another open volume. " 'One might think a good way to trace a poison is by its symptoms, but this has proved most difficult, for many symptoms overlap.' "

"I know," said Brian, sighing. "I read that, too."

"Sweet clover," murmured Numbles. "Hey, it says here that there's something in clover that can make the blood stop clotting, if it's got a fungus, the clover, I mean. There's lots of clover around here."

"Not in my grandfather's fields," said Brian. "He clears it out, just for that reason."

Darcy was peering over Numbles's shoulder. "What a lot of poisonous plants! Sheesh—ordinary things. Irises, hydrangeas—we've got those. Some ferns . . . But I bet the vet would've known if it was any of those, huh?"

"Cyanide," said Brian, skimming aloud. "Staggering. Loss of consciousness. Whoops—acts rapidly. And I guess from what it says here, it would've shown up in an autopsy." He looked up. "Ditto strychnine and arsenic, at least I think so. And as your book said, Darcy, it's hard to pin them down from the symptoms. We don't know much about those, anyway." He stood up and put on a businesslike, inquiring face. "Excuse me, cow, but do you have a stomachache?

Acute abdominal pain? Nausea? A burning sensation in your mouth? Do you feel exhausted, as if you can't breathe?" He sat down again and said, "But since all those poisons would probably show up in an autopsy, I guess we don't have to worry about asking the cows about their symptoms."

"If the silly things could talk," said Darcy, "they could tell us who poisoned them in the first place, couldn't they? Then the kind of poison wouldn't matter so much. Oh-oh." She jerked her head toward the front of the table; the blond librarian was coming toward them.

"May I help you with something?" she asked pleasantly, and then her eyes fell on the pages open in front of them.

"No thanks," Darcy said sweetly. "We're just doing some research into poisons. Trying to find one that could make a cow sick enough to die, and not leave any trace." She batted her eyelashes. "You don't know of one, do you?"

"Well, I—" the librarian's hand fluttered to her throat. "I don't . . ."

"My grandfather's cows," said Brian, feeling sorry for her, "might be being poisoned. So we're trying to find out what kind of poison it could be."

"Oh," said the librarian. "But wouldn't the vet know? Surely he'd . . ."

"Apparently not," Numbles said. "He's done autopsies and everything. That's why we're looking for something that doesn't leave a trace."

"Curare!" Brian sprang to his feet and reached for the C volume of the nearest encyclopedia. "Why didn't I think of that? Holmes mentions it; it can be deadly and I think he even says someplace that it's hard to trace—here it is."

They all bent over the book, the librarian included this time, and read:

CURARE: A dark brown or black gum made from various combinations of South American plants, including the vine *Chondodendron tomentosum*, and used by Indians to stun or kill animals. The drug is employed as a muscle relaxant in some surgical procedures. When curare is used as a poison, death is caused by failure of the respiratory system.

Native hunters apply curare to the end of an arrow or dart, and fire it into an animal with a blowgun, the apparatus commonly being aimed at the animal's neck. Death is rapid if the dose is large enough.

"Which means," Brian said slowly, "that it might not be rapid if the dose were small." He pointed to the words *failure of the respiratory system* and said, "That calf was having a hard time breathing."

"There's nothing about its being hard to trace," said Numbles skeptically. "Are you sure Holmes said that? Besides, who's to say it can't be traced now? Conan Doyle wrote those stories about a hundred years ago, after all. A lot of them, anyway."

"But the book does say curare's used to kill animals," Darcy put in.

"And it can be given from a distance," Brian added. "That works."

"It seems a little exotic," said the librarian, who had been thumbing through some of the other books and was now looking at the curare article again. "I mean, who around here would have curare? You're sure it's not a native plant that's doing it, something the cows just got into? That happens sometimes, you know. Or a snake."

"No," said Numbles patiently. "It's very unlikely it's a snake."

Brian had closed the book; he wasn't listening to any of them. Okay, Holmes, he was saying in his mind. Maybe it's only a two-pipe problem now. Or no-pipe. So what if it's a farfetched idea? It's too good a one to pass up. The first thing we have to do is find where there's a source of curare . . .

"Simple!" he said aloud, jumping to his feet. "Or, as they say in the movies, 'Elementary, my dear Watson!' "

He ran out of the library, closely followed by the other two, leaving the bewildered librarian standing beside the litter of books they'd left behind them.

POISON HUNTERS

THE GROVE HILL DRUGGIST insisted that curare would be well-nigh impossible to get hold of in rural Vermont. The plants, for one thing, would have to be imported if someone were trying to make curare on the sly, and legitimate buyers would have to order the manufactured drug from a pharmaceutical company. Certainly no one had gotten any curare through him in all the forty years he'd been a pharmacist. Besides, there were all kinds of government regulations.

Momentarily discouraged, Brian said goodbye to Numbles and Darcy and dragged himself slowly home.

Grandpop was standing glumly with two other men at the edge of his far pasture when Brian arrived.

"I've got an old bike you can use," Grandpop offered as Brian draped himself tiredly around a fence post. "If that walk to the village is getting to you. Good game?"

"Great," Brian answered—but his eyes, like his

grandfather's, were on the large black and white body lying beside the fence. "Another?" he asked, trying to see if there was a wound in the cow's neck that could have been made by a dart from a blowgun.

Grandpop nodded. "Been off a couple of days," he told Brian, "like the others. I got another one sickening, too."

"Like I was saying, Sam," said one of the two other men — short and stubby, in a frayed tweed jacket and a porkpie hat. "I don't see how we can handle your milk any more. I'm sorry, and I know what it'll do to you, but . . ."

"You said there's no sign of anything in the milk, Greerson," said the other man, who, from the black bag on the ground beside him, Brian surmised was the vet.

"We haven't *found* anything in the milk," said Mr. Greerson. He must be the man from the milk co-op, Brian thought, who Grandmom had said wanted to talk to Grandpop. "But we can't risk there being something we haven't found, can we?" He turned back to Grandpop. "First kid that takes sick, whether it's your milk or not, that'll be the end of your business once word gets out about your cows. Our business, too, could be. Better to prevent that than let it happen, right?" He slapped Grandpop on the back. "Soon's we get to the bottom of this," he said heartily, "we'll take you right back into the co-op. Come along, Jaffrey," he said to the vet. "I'll help you load 'er up."

Brian watched silently along with his grandfather while the two men attached ropes to the dead cow's body and hoisted it into the truck the vet had waiting. Again, he tried to see if there was a wound in the cow's neck, but he couldn't really tell from a distance, and he didn't want to annoy Grandpop by being obvious about it, when Grandpop was sure deliberate poisoning wasn't the cause of death.

When the cow was loaded, Grandpop turned abruptly without saying a word, and walked toward the barn, his shoulders sagging and his step slow and heavy.

I've got to do something, Brian thought, before he really falls apart.

And curare's my only lead. Only idea, anyway.

It still seemed possible that someone had found a clandestine source of curare, or was making it, even if the pharmacist did say the plants would have to be imported. Or using some other exotic poison that was equally hard to trace.

He walked idly over to the fence, and stood there looking down at the weeds that lined it.

I wonder, he thought suddenly, if the plants—that *Chondodendron*-whatever vine and the others needed for making curare—could grow in Vermont in the summer. Then the poisoner would only have to have smuggled in seeds. Besides, maybe a dart from a blowgun isn't the only way to poison a cow with curare.

What if someone deliberately planted the natural

ingredients for curare where the cows would eat them — and what if the county agent's crew over-looked them because they were hunting for parasites instead of plants? That might even explain why most of Grandpop's cows were sick for a few days before they died and why the calf died more quickly. It would probably take fewer plants to kill a calf.

Brian walked methodically around the edge of the far pasture, examining the vegetation there for any-thing that looked unusual, especially vines. It would take hours, he soon realized, to search the whole field carefully, and then there'd be the near pasture to search as well, if nothing turned up in this one.

Still, that was just the kind of painstaking search Holmes would undertake. Darcy ought to be good at that, with her "total concentration." If only she and Numbles would agree to help . . .

"Sure," said Darcy easily the next day, standing on the bank of the small woodland pond where they'd agreed to meet for a swim; Cadge was sniffing along the shore. "I don't have much else to do except soft-ball. Numbles hasn't either, except for feeding his critters. Do you, Numb?"

"Well," said Numbles, hiking his bathing suit up around his fleshy stomach, "no, actually. Besides, I just might find a specimen or two in those fields."

"Thanks," said Brian gratefully. "I don't think I could even begin to do the whole thing myself." He paused a moment, then went on carefully, hoping he wasn't going too far. "Maybe we should look for blowgun wounds in the cows' necks, too, just in case. And talk to the vet and the county agent and the co-op guy about poisons in general. We might as well cover everything."

"Numbles'd be best for the talking part," said Darcy. "He's good at dealing with adults; heck, he even sounds like one half the time."

"I could do the search part," Brian said, "since I sort of know the cows." He turned hopefully to Darcy.

"Which leaves the plants for me." Darcy made a face. "Yuck. It's a good thing we have botany at that stupid school I go to." She snapped her towel like a whip. "Poison hunters it is. Hey—I bet we're going to crack this case wide open! But first I'm going for a swim. Last one in!" She ran into the pond with Cadge close behind her, and made a splashy surface dive as soon as she was deep enough.

Brian followed and Numbles walked slowly in after them. "Ah," he said, easing himself into the water, turning onto his back, and gazing up at the sky, "this is the life. Rest, relaxation, the warm sun beating down on one's head . . ."

"And belly," said Darcy, splashing water onto Numbles's white stomach, which protruded quite a bit above the waterline. "You're going to get a belly burn if you don't watch out."

"Oh, don't be crude, Darcy Dixie," said Numbles,

whereupon Darcy splashed him again and for the next few minutes the two of them, plus Cadge, were hidden behind a wall of dancing water.

"Enough!" Numbles gasped, standing, water streaming from his face. "You win, Darce. I'm going over to the other side and look for frogs. There was a *Rana septentrionalis* here the last time I came, and I want to see if it's still around. I'll thank you to stay on this side if you're going to be noisy."

"Okay, professor," said Darcy and, turning to Brian, she asked, "how about that race?"

He beat her easily three times.

NEEDLES IN HAYSTACKS

NUMBLES RAN HIS FINGER under the collar of his clean white shirt, trying to mop up the sweat that had collected there. A fan whirled the hot air around in the milk co-op office's waiting room, but somehow it only made him more conscious of the heat that pressed down on him from all sides. Outdoors, at least, there was more space for the heat to spread out in.

"Edward Crane?" A tired-looking short man in a rumpled tweed jacket emerged from an inside office. "Ed?" He looked right past Numbles, even though there was no one else in the room.

Numbles stood up and cleared his throat. "I'm Edward Crane, Junior, sir," he said politely.

The man smiled damply; how anyone could wear a wool jacket on such a hot day was beyond Numbles. "Yes," said the man, "I see. You do look a bit like your dad. Where is he—parking? We don't usually get that crowded here."

"My dad's not with me," said Numbles, with a certain amount of relish. "I'm the Edward Crane who called. You must be Mr. Greerson."

Mr. Greerson did not look pleased. "Yes," he said, "I am. But I'm afraid I haven't got much time. I . . ."

"Your secretary said you were free all this morning," said Numbles smoothly, "when I called yesterday to make the appointment."

"Yes, well," said Mr. Greerson, gesturing Numbles into his inner office, "something's come up. You know how—no, I guess you don't. Oh, come along, boy, have a seat." Gruffly, he motioned Numbles toward a faded red armchair in front of a desk piled high with papers, folders, and pamphlets bearing titles like *A New Method of Homogenization*, *Milking Machines from A to Z*, *Bovine Brucelosis*, and *Bacteria and Milk*.

"What was it you wanted?" he asked Numbles. "School paper? But school's not open yet."

"No." Numbles let his annoyance at the man's patronizing attitude begin to show a little. "Nothing like that." He had already decided he'd get nowhere if he told the truth. Who'd give that kind of specific information to a kid, especially during an ongoing investigation? So he said, "I'm in the local chapter of MENSA, and we're doing a study for the government on milk-borne diseases and parasites, especially any ailment affecting the bloodstream." He leaned across the desk and asked indulgently, "You're familiar with MENSA? The national organization for people with

IQs of genius level and beyond? No age minimum, of course; there can't be, you see, for intelligence has nothing to do with years." Phew, he thought, I wonder if that's how those smarties really talk.

If it wasn't, Mr. Greerson didn't seem aware of it, nor did he seem to suspect that Numbles himself knew next to nothing about MENSA. He did stare at Numbles for an awkward moment, but then he cleared his throat and said in an embarrassed way, "I see. What government agency was it you said you were doing this for?"

"I didn't say," Numbles replied politely. "And I'm afraid I can't. It's all very confidential, as will be anything you tell me. But in case you're skeptical . . ." He pulled out his wallet and extracted a fake MENSA ID card he'd made earlier. Praying that Mr. Greerson had never seen the real thing—if indeed MENSA members even had ID cards—he handed it across the desk, and Mr. Greerson, after studying it for an excruciatingly long few seconds, handed it back. "I see," he said again. "Well, now. What was it specifically that you needed to know?"

It felt to Darcy a little like the old boring times when she'd had to gather wildflowers with her Aunt Amanda, and it felt a lot like looking for a needle in a haystack, as her mom would say—but at least her search had an important purpose. She had started right after an early breakfast and had already been around the entire perimeter of the far pasture, whose large L-shape had grass-bordered woods on two sides. Dirt paths and Mr. Larrabee's driveway formed three more sides, and the road edged the remaining one. Luckily, Mr. Larrabee was off cutting hay in a field he didn't use for grazing; she wouldn't have to answer any awkward questions. And the cows were in the near pasture today, so she wouldn't have to work around them.

Along the road turned out to be the most interesting place to search, for the plants there were a combination of field plants and woods ones, mixed in with strays from the edge of the road and from the Larrabees' garden.

So far, though, there was nothing in the old pillowcase she'd gotten from her mother to use as a collecting bag; she hadn't seen anything she couldn't identify. Pretty good, Darce, she thought; Miss Fisher would be proud.

Miss Fisher taught botany at Darcy's school in Hunt Valley, Maryland.

Wait'll the other kids hear we caught a murderer this summer, she thought with satisfaction, moving carefully out into the field for the length of the yardstick she carried with her, after fastening one end of a ball of string to the fence that bordered the road. String, she figured, would keep her going in a straight line; she'd be able to see if she wavered.

If we catch him, she thought, eyes down, walking slowly. Queen Anne's lace, alfalfa, Kentucky bluegrass, red fescue, clover—hadn't Mr. Larrabee tried to get rid of all the clover because it was harmful to cows? What had the book said about it? Poisonous if eaten in enough quantity? No. Fungus—stops blood from clotting, that was it. Still, that would obviously be harmful to cows.

And here was a sizable patch, right at her feet.

She bent down and carefully picked a handful, put it into a small plastic bag, and then dropped it into her collecting bag, just as she heard the hum of Mr. Larrabee's tractor coming closer.

Brian, in the near pasture with the herd, whistled to Cadge, and signaled him to move yet another cow away from her companions. It was tedious work, cutting them out one at a time, and he'd already been at it for hours, but it was a pleasure to watch the dog's lithe body twisting and crouching, driving and darting. Cadge worked with every bit as much concentration as Darcy when she pitched, and with a smoothness rivaling any swimmer's. He's an athlete, too, Brian thought, as the cow lumbered toward him and Cadge snaked behind, belly to the ground, keeping her on course.

"So, Bossy; so, my girl," Brian crooned as he'd heard Grandpop do, and he ran his hand over her flank; she twisted her head around and eyed Cadge nervously.

"Down, Cadge," Brian said, and the dog dropped instantly.

Brian pulled the small stepladder he'd borrowed from the kitchen closer to the cow and climbed it, examining her neck, shoulders, and flanks, first the left and then, switching the ladder, the right.

Nothing. Smoother than smooth. The short hairs lay even and undisturbed, forming a white background with a black map spread across the cow's shoulders. Not a mark.

Of course, this cow didn't show the slightest sign of weakness. Holmes would look at all the cows, though, just in case. And this way, Brian thought, I might even catch one at the very first stages.

With renewed enthusiasm, Brian got down off the ladder and gave the cow a light spank on her rear. "Come by, Cadge," he called, giving the traditional command for sending a dog clockwise around a herd, and directed him to single out the next cow.

"I'm sorry," said Mr. Greerson, leaning back in his chair, "that I can't give you any more information than that." He pushed a small pile of pamphlets about cattle diseases to Numbles over his desk top. "These may be some help, and they have good bibliographies at the end, so they may lead you to more information. That hypothetical case is interesting, though," he went on. "The one where the cows died of no apparent cause but weakness. As a matter of fact"—was his look the slightest bit suspicious?—"it's not so hypothetical.

There's a farmer near here who has a similar situation."

"Oh?" said Numbles carefully. "Is there?"

"Yes. Sam Larrabee, down off the main road. Big dairy farmer, one of our best. I'm surprised you don't know him. I suppose it doesn't hurt to mention it; it's pretty common knowledge by now."

"Oh, yes," said Numbles. "Come to think of it, I did hear something, you're right."

"Well, you might want to give him a call. His case is much as you described. We've run every test we know on the milk from that farm, and there's no sign of contamination. But of course we can't accept the milk, even so."

"Of course not."

"Nor have we ever run across a similar disease in all our years of being in the milk business."

"What about," asked Numbles casually, "poison?"

"Very doubtful. Very doubtful indeed. The vet's tested extensively, and there's not a trace . . ."

"Aren't there some poisons, though, that don't leave a trace? And that are administered directly into the bloodstream? Would that show up in the milk?"

"It would depend, I suppose," said Mr. Greerson, "on the poison itself and on—oh, I don't know. It shouldn't show up in the milk, should it, if it enters through the bloodstream? I'm not a vet, though; perhaps you'd better speak to Dr. Jaffrey. And the county agent; he's been looking into it, too."

"Yes," said Numbles, standing up. "As a matter of fact, I'm about to."

There was a bit more clover, but nothing else of interest until Darcy came to a patch of squashed-looking grass not far from one corner of the field that faced the new pasture. The grass was trampled, as if cows had passed across it many times.

She frowned, stooping. Now why would a whole herd of cows spend so much time in a small rectangle roughly six feet long and three or so feet wide that they flattened it more than any of the grass around it?

Wait—not quite. A wide strip of grass running like a path from the trampled patch to the gate was also bent over, more packed down at the edges than in the middle. It was almost as if at least a few cows had walked around and around in the flattened place, trampling the grass there—and then gone to the gate along the strip, with most of them walking along the edges.

I don't know a whole lot about cows, Darcy said to herself, kneeling to examine the rectangle of packed-down grass more closely, but what I've seen of them tells me that isn't too likely.

She fluffed up some of the grass with her hands, parted it—and then bent closer, for a brownish powder clung to one small cluster of blades in a spot only a couple of inches in diameter.

Not powder, really. It looked more as if something liquid had dried there.

Darcy whipped out her jackknife and trimmed a neat bunch for her collecting bag.

Brian wiped his forehead; the sun was well past its noon position, and heat rose in waves from the distant road. The cows had bunched together at the far end of the field, in the shade. There was only one more to go—a good thing, for even Cadge was flagging now.

The last cow was like all the others, without a mark on her.

Wearily, Brian patted and released her and then, picking up the stepladder and calling Cadge, crossed the field to the gate—where he almost crashed smack into Cadge, who had run ahead but then stopped abruptly.

Flies buzzed by the side of the driveway; under them, Brian saw a large black and white body.

He went through the gate at a run; Grandpop hadn't said anything about a new victim. But maybe he'd just come back from haying, found it, and was inside now calling the vet. Still—how had it gotten out of the pasture?

And which pasture had it been in?

He cringed a little as he put down the stepladder and knelt by the cow's massive carcass. A whine from Cadge made him turn; the dog was circling the body warily, giving it a wide berth. His neck hair bristled and a low growl rumbled in his throat.

"It's just a cow, Cadge," Brian said uneasily; hadn't Cadge acted funny with that dead calf a few days ago? But why—could he smell the poison?

Tentatively, Brian reached out and touched the body. The side of the neck that he could see was fine, smooth and unblemished, like that of all the other cows. Was he really going to have to turn it over?

Holmes would.

But Holmes, Brian thought, tugging at the animal while Cadge whined annoyingly in the background, would have hailed some passing country bumpkin to help; somehow he never had to get his hands really dirty on a case.

Well, that wasn't quite true, Brian realized, trying futilely to haul the cow's front legs around. In "The Hound of the Baskervilles," he spent hours out on a barren moor. But he did always have Watson do a lot of legwork.

Brian gave up on the idea of turning the cow over, and instead tried picking up her head. He was able to lift it just enough, finally, to peer underneath.

The neck on the other side was not unblemished; he saw that instantly, although one would have to be looking closely for the mark to see it.

Halfway down, the hairs were upright in two spots.

And when he probed with his fingers, Brian found two small scab-covered wounds hidden under the hair.

BLOOD ON THE GRASS

"THE CO-OP GUY and the county agent were no help at all," panted Numbles, running up to where Brian was still staring down at the dead cow and Cadge was shivering a few feet away, "but the vet says that most poisons only show up—holy cow!"

Darcy, who had come up at about the same time, made an odd noise. "Well, I wouldn't say *holy*, exactly," she remarked, "but dead, certainly. What's up, Bri? Anything?"

"Possibly," he said, lifting the cow's head again so they could look underneath at the wounds. "But why a dart from a blowgun would make *two* marks beats me. Unless the blowgun was fired twice—but why, if curare's so lethal? I remember Grandpop saying the vet mentioned finding scratches and insect bites, but insects don't ordinarily make two bites, do they, Numb?"

"Not that I know of. Maybe sometimes. I don't know. It's not my field."

Darcy whistled. "Hey, listen," she said. "I don't know how this fits, or even if it does, but . . ." She told them about the beaten-down grass and the brownish spot.

"For what it's worth," said Numbles, "which may be nothing, Dr. Jaffrey, who I saw after I left the milk guy . . ."

"The milkman," quipped Darcy.

Numbles poked her.

"Ow!"

"I was saying," Numbles continued severely, "that Dr. Jaffrey told me that most—well, lots of—poisons don't show up in tests unless you test specifically for them. Like you have to know what you're looking for, I guess, before you start testing."

"So even if there were curare in a cow," said Brian, "and even if I'm wrong about it and it *is* traceable, it wouldn't show up unless you tested for it. Right?"

"I asked him about curare, but he laughed."

"Laughed?"

"Yeah. He said I'd been reading too many comic books. That no one outside of South American natives uses the stuff for poison, and then mostly just in the movies. He also said that at least the curare that's used in surgery has to be given intravenously, so our plant theory's probably wrong. It might not even be poisonous if it's swallowed."

Numbles bent and examined the cow more closely; the others joined him. "The vet also laughed at the idea of anyone's using medicinal curare as poison," Numbles went on, "although I finally got him to say it was possible. But he agreed with the druggist that it would be hard to get. He said even if someone swiped some out of a hospital pharmacy they probably wouldn't use a blowgun for it, but a needle, and they're hard to swipe, too. And he said no legitimate medical person would abuse it."

"Yeah, but how about an illegitimate medical person?" said Brian. "Anyone can commit a crime. And anything can be swiped if someone wants to swipe it badly enough." He pointed at the cow. "But anyway, her wound wasn't made with a hypo."

"It's small enough," said Darcy. "Well, almost,"

"Almost isn't good enough," answered Brian. "How many two-pronged hypos have you seen?" He stood up and brushed off his hands; Cadge stood up, too, as if eager to go. "I think my curare theory's wrong," he announced, trying not to sound as discouraged as he felt. "Let's go see your grass, Darcy. Maybe that'll give us some kind of lead we can use."

"Yuck." Darcy looked back at the cow as they left. "The mark's like pincers, sort of, like tiny fire tongs. Or"—she tugged Numbles's arm—"like teeth. Very sharp fangs. Hey, no, wait a minute, guys! Really." She planted herself in front of them. "Come on. How *about* teeth? I mean, okay, Numbles, you say there aren't very many poisonous snakes around here. But all it'd take would be one. And maybe—maybe it wouldn't keep coming back on its own. But suppose"—her eyes widened and her voice dropped—"suppose someone made it come back? Suppose someone had a fancy foreign snake and, you know, used it to . . ."

"Oh, stow it, Darcy," Numbles snapped impatiently. "We've been all through that."

"Not quite," said Brian, seeing Darcy's crestfallen look. "The idea of a foreign snake someone's brought here is a good one. But remember, the vet also tested for snake venom, and he didn't find anything." He patted Darcy on the shoulder. "Nice try, though. Now come on," he said as they went in through the far pasture gate. "Where's that patch of grass?"

"He might not have tested for the right snake venom," Darcy grumbled stubbornly as she closed the gate behind them and pointed to the wide strip of bent-over grass. "See—this bit goes from the gate all the way to the brown stuff." She led them along the edge of the path in the grass. Cadge, who'd been trotting along beside Brian, followed, but sat down some distance from the stained spot when they got to it.

"I cut a little of it," said Darcy, "for my collecting bag. But there's plenty left."

"Blood," said Brian, as soon as he'd knelt beside the rectangular patch and examined the brownish spot. "I bet it's dried blood."

"Very good, Holmes," said Numbles, looking over his shoulder. "I do believe you're right."

"Okay," said Darcy, "but then who's it from? And how did the grass get all squashed? And on the path, why's the grass more squashed at the edges? Tell me that if you're so smart."

"It's easy." Brian stood up, feeling more confident than he had all day. "The cow was killed here," he said, indicating the trampled rectangle with his foot. "Or she died here, anyway. The cause of death was the wound in her neck. The brownish stuff is her blood. The grass here is squashed because she lay here for a while after she fell. And I think the path of squashed grass going off to the gate is where someone dragged her off the field, to the side of the driveway. Since the grass is more squashed at the edges than in the middle, as you noticed, Darcy, I bet whoever moved her used a tractor; the treads would have done the most squashing. Of course I didn't notice any rope marks on the cow, but after all, I was looking at her neck."

"She has to have been removed before Darcy got to this part of the field," said Numbles, "but she can't have lain by the driveway for very long or she'd probably have been stiff. But she was still flexible. No rigor mortis."

"True," said Brian. "Very good, Watson. My guess is that Grandpop had her in this field in the first place because she was already sick. Did you hear a tractor or notice a cow here, Darcy, when you arrived?"

"I heard a tractor, but I didn't see any cow."

"That shoots that, then, Holmes," said Numbles.

"I don't think so," Brian answered. "Where did you look for plants first, Darcy?"

"Around the edge. I didn't get over here till the end."

"Good," said Brian triumphantly. "So the cow could already have been lying here when you came into the field. The grass around the squashed place is tall enough to hide a cow's body, especially if you aren't looking for one. So if my theory's right so far," he went on, pacing, "Grandpop must've come back to check on the cow when Darcy and I were both too busy and too far away to notice. He found her dead, here on the grass her body had squashed down, hitched her to the tractor, and dragged her out to the drive-way, making the path. And of course the wound could've bled after she fell, and then the blood could've dried, making the scab."

"All right, Holmes!" said Numbles, with obvious admiration.

"If you two are Holmes and Watson," said Darcy petulantly, "then who am I?"

"Mrs. Hudson," said Numbles. "Holmes's house-keeper."

"Oh, no," said Darcy. "No way."

"Inspector Lestrade," offered Brian. "From Scot-land Yard. He used to come up with a good idea now and then."

"Mostly then," Numbles said under his breath to

Brian. More loudly, he said, "Well, but Holmes, we still don't know who killed the cow, do we? Or what killed her—the murder weapon, I mean."

Brian shook his head, then knelt and studied the rectangle of flattened grass again, wishing he had that magnifying glass Basil Rathbone carried when he played Holmes in the movies.

"You've got a good idea, Bri," said Darcy finally. "But it just doesn't go far enough. Like Numbles said, what killed her? If it's not poison . . ."

"I know," said Brian. "We're back to a three-pipe problem. The only thing I can think of is loss of blood—remember, the vet said low blood volume. But it seems to me that if the cow bled that much, there'd be a lot more blood on the ground."

"Look at Cadge," said Darcy suddenly.

Brian turned. Cadge was lying about ten yards away from them, panting; he was as hunched into himself as he'd been near the dead cow at the edge of the driveway.

"Cadge," called Numbles. "Come here, boy."

But Cadge didn't budge.

"Why, Cadge," said Brian. "Bad dog. Come. Come!"

The dog whimpered and rolled over onto his back, like a puppy at its most submissive.

Brian frowned. What would make a perfectly trained dog like Cadge disobey?

There had to be a logical explanation. Maybe the smell of blood?

Darcy went up to the dog, who lolled his tongue

out and let her rub his stomach. "What is it, Cadge?" she asked softly. "What's the matter, boy?" She tugged at his collar. "Come on, come over to where we are. Come on." She slapped her hip and ran ahead a step or two.

Cadge rolled onto his front again, and wagged his tail, but he still wouldn't move.

Decisively, Brian went to the dog. First he scratched his ears and patted his head, saying, "Come on, old boy. I'm your pal Brian, remember? I wouldn't make you do anything dangerous, would I? Now come on." When again the dog wouldn't move, Brian stooped, picked him up, and carried him toward the squashed grass.

Cadge, with a mighty wiggle, jumped down from Brian's arms and streaked back to his "safe" spot, tail between his legs, and lay there trembling.

GOING BATTY

"TONIGHT AFTER CHORES," said Grandpop at breakfast the next morning—he had indeed moved the dead cow with the tractor, he'd told Brian the night before—"I'm going to see if I can clear the bats out of the barn. There've been more than usual this summer, and I don't like 'em around. Want to help?"

"Sure," said Brian. Then it hit him. "Grandpop," he said excitedly, thinking of Darcy's suggesting that the cows had been bitten by something, "could that be it? I mean, bats carry diseases, don't they? Rabies and stuff?"

"Indeed they do, Brian," said Grandmom, "but did you ever hear of a rabid cow?"

"Rampaging through the streets," said Grandpop, laughing, "frothing at the mouth, biting everyone in sight, with the dog catcher in hot pursuit! Sorry, Brian." He wiped his eyes; Brian, rather hurt, pushed his plate away. Grandpop patted Brian's hand. "No offense, son. It's just that everything's been so tense lately, a good laugh is what we all needed. The bats around here eat insects; I never heard of one biting a cow. They're a nuisance, though, and I should have cleared them out long before now. Why don't you see if your friends want to help, too? After supper—there'll still be some time before it gets really dark. We can make a party out of it. A bat-clearing party."

Numbles agreed readily, and Darcy a little less so. That evening they met Grandmom and Brian in the barn, where Grandpop was passing out instructions and what looked like butterfly nets. "Now remember," he told them, "bats aren't supposed to be able to see worth beans, but their hearing's terrific. They find their way by sonar; that's why they dart around so much. And they're fragile. We don't want to kill them, just move them. There's a cave in the woods where I think most of them come from, and I want to transport them back there. The idea is to catch them one at a time and put them in here."

He displayed a large cage not unlike a turtle trap Brian had seen at Numbles's house, with a long cone-like opening that was narrow on the inside and wide on the outside.

"Now let's get going before they get suspicious. Or lively; they get active as it gets dark. I suppose we really should have done this earlier in the day, but there's too much else to do then." Grandpop picked up the cage and, handing his net to Brian, started up a ladder at one end of the barn. Brian followed, with Numbles, Darcy, and Grandmom close behind.

The bats lived in the top loft, and were hanging upside-down from the rafters like black gloves out to dry.

Grandpop was right about their number; Brian gulped as he handed Grandpop back his net and saw how many there were. It's probably only forty or fifty, he reasoned—but it looked like a lot more. In any case, it was a lot of bats for five people to catch. Ten per person, Brian figured, going up to his first one and slipping his net under it carefully so it wouldn't wake up. At Grandpop's suggestion, he gave the net a sharp twist and the bat dropped neatly and harmlessly into it, emitting a feeble, sleepy squeak.

Brian laughed. "Hey, this is easy!" he said to Numbles, who was working just to his left; he moved confidently to the next bat.

Bat after bat followed, as the five crept stealthily along under the rafters for what seemed like forever. Several were hard to catch, and toward the end, Grandpop had to light his barn lantern against the encroaching darkness.

"There," said Grandpop finally. "I think that's the whole bunch of 'em." He began collecting nets.

"What's that, Mr. Larrabee?" Darcy asked when he came to her.

"What?"

"That." She pointed to something hanging above a

pile of dirt in a far corner of the loft; the dirt seemed oddly out of place, and the bat that Brian finally made out in the dim light was so much bigger than the others that he felt sure he'd have noticed it if it had been there before. It was so big it looked more like a black cape than a glove.

When Grandpop approached, the bat opened its tiny red eyes and looked straight at him.

"Ugh," said Darcy. "That one looks mean! Big and mean. Don't tell me it can't see just fine!" She edged toward the ladder that led down to the floor below.

"Careful, Mr. Larrabee." Numbles took his net back and held it at the ready.

"Grandpop," began Brian, "maybe . . ."

But Grandpop was intent on the bat. "Stand back, everyone," he ordered. He swooped at the bat, but the bat, whose wingspan was like a large hawk's, swooped back at him, rising only just short of hitting him and knocking him down. "Dang beast!" Grandpop shouted, brandishing his net, as Darcy picked up a pitchfork and Brian looked wildly around for something similar. Wisps of hay flew up as the bat darted around the five of them, its wing tips knocking down cobwebs and churning up dust; it flew so fast and so erratically there was no way any of them could catch it. They all pivoted helplessly and flailed about with their arms as it changed direction.

"Watch out!" Numbles shouted as the bat flew at Grandmom, who screamed and covered her head with trembling hands.

It's just a bat, Brian kept telling himself, but he felt like screaming, too, and vaulting down the ladder. From the look on Numbles's and Darcy's faces, he was sure they felt the same.

The bat perched for a moment on the hay bale and looked from one of them to the other, as if deciding which one to fly at next.

"It's weird," whispered Numbles, "but it looks— well, *smart*. Look at those eyes, Bri, look . . ."

"Steady now," said Grandpop, creeping forward, holding his net out like a lance. "Everyone stay very still . . ."

"Oooooh," screamed Grandmom as the bat dove at her once more. "Oh, *shoo!*" She hit at the bat's wing with the handle of her net as it passed.

With an angry shriek, the bat flew toward the peak of the roof and perched on a rafter, from which it glared down at Grandmom and hissed.

"You've made an enemy there, Jessie," said Grandpop shakily. "And now he's too far out of reach and not likely to come down. I don't think we'd better provoke him any more tonight." He began collecting nets again. "I guess one bat in the barn's a lot better than fifty, even if he is a big one. Anyone want to come with me to the cave? I know it's late, but the other bats are getting pretty restless. I think we'd better get rid of 'em in a hurry. I just hope they don't all come trooping back. You okay, Jessie?"

Grandmom was sitting on a hay bale in one corner. "I—yes," she said. "I think so. My hand's sore, though, from when I hit him. Funny, he was harder than I expected."

"You probably hit bone," said Grandpop, helping her up. "And from the look of it, you did more harm to him than he did to you." He glanced up at the bat, which was licking its wing and moving it slowly, as an injured person tests a sore limb.

Numbles was tugging at Brian's arm; the others were already heading down the ladder with the full cage. "Holmes," he said in an undertone, his eyes, like Brian's, on the sinister creature, "did you ever hear of *vampire* bats? They spread disease worse than ordinary bats, as I remember, and they bite cows. Eat their blood, actually, which could account for that low blood volume."

"Good thinking, Watson," Brian said, his eyes on the bat on the rafter; it was still nursing its wing and staring evilly down at them—him especially, he felt. "Are vampire bats larger than other bats, I wonder?"

"I don't know. I'd have to look it up."

"Numbles!" Darcy was calling from below. "Brian! Come on! We're ready to go."

It was a small cave, smaller than Brian had envisioned, nestled among huge slabs of gray rock in a forest that looked, in the eerie light from Grandpop's lantern, like something out of a fantasy movie.

"Sheesh!" exclaimed Darcy as the little group stepped inside the cave. "It's *cold* in here!"

"It'll get colder," said Grandpop. He switched on a large flashlight. "Not to mention darker."

Grandmom slipped out of her light sweater. "Here, dear. Put this on."

"Oh, it's okay, Mrs. Larrabee," Darcy said, sounding embarrassed. "Really. It just takes getting used to, that's all."

Numbles, carrying the full cage with Brian, nudged him; ahead, where Grandpop was shining his light, was a rough rock ledge, from which were hanging dozens of bats. A few stirred sleepily, and one or two flew toward the entrance emitting a high-pitched twittering. Brian realized that he'd been vaguely conscious of the sound ever since they'd stepped inside.

"Bat friends and relations," said Grandpop. "Getting active now that it's dark. I think we can set our prisoners free now." He motioned the boys to put the cage down, and then he unfastened the catch himself and removed the entrance cone. When the bats didn't move, he upended the cage, so most of them fell out. One small plump one lingered; Grandpop prodded it gently with the flashlight and finally it squealed indignantly and waddled away, a bit like a spoiled, overfed child.

Darcy shivered and moved closer to Grandmom. Brian wiped unexplainably cold sweat off his forehead. But Numbles, whistling, was already turning over rocks. "There ought to be plenty of salamanders in here," he remarked. "It's dark and damp enough."

"Umm," said Grandpop. "I believe there are. What about this fellah, for instance?" He flashed his light onto a small rock-colored creature.

"Desmognathus fuscus fuscus!" cried Numbles excitedly, snatching it up. "Great! At least I think that's what it is; they're hard to identify. Look, Brian, see the little yellow spots? They're round now, but if I've got the right animal, they'll be less obvious when it gets older. This is a young one, I'd say. There must be running water somewhere in this cave. Look at the jaw line . . ."

Brian looked, trying to concentrate as Numbles pointed out the little creature's fine points.

"There's another," said Darcy. "At least I think there is. I just put my hand on something soft."

Grandmom chuckled and Grandpop shined his light—on Grandmom's left hand. She wiggled her index finger and said, "How do you like my tail?"

"Very nice," said Darcy. "Especially the hard pointy bit at the end. What do you call that?"

"Looks hard as nails," said Numbles, and Brian was finally able to laugh.

"It must be time to go." Grandpop picked up the empty cage. "When we start mistaking each other for salamanders, I know we've had enough. It's high time for a little nourishment. Who's for some nice juicy homemade blueberry pie?"

The next morning, Brian went sleepily downstairs at the usual time to find a very out-of-sorts Grandpop frying bacon. "Morning," Grandpop grumbled. "Two slices? Three? A hundred?"

Brian grinned. "A hundred sounds good," he said. "But I'll settle for three or four. Where's Grandmom?"

"In bed, not feeling well. She had bad dreams all night, and didn't sleep much between them. Neither did I, what with all her tossing and turning. I think I'll sleep in the guest room tonight. I've got cows to tend and I can't afford to lie around in bed all day."

Brian let that go. "Toast?" he asked, reaching for the bread box. "Grandmom want anything?"

"Nope. Says the thought of food makes her feel sick."

"Maybe she ate something bad." Brian popped two slices of bread into the toaster.

"She didn't eat anything we didn't eat," snapped Grandpop, lifting the bacon out of the pan slice by slice and draining it on paper towels.

"No, I guess not." Brian took out plates, mugs, and silverware and began setting the table.

It was a dismal breakfast, and a dismal morning to boot, with a gray sky and occasional drizzly rain — not *real* rain, as Darcy said when Brian met her and Numbles at the library after a sloppy ride on Grandpop's old bike, but a meager half rain, played out but apparently not quite ready to stop.

Numbles was cheerful, though, as if like some of his reptiles he was absorbing the moisture through his skin and being refreshed by it. "Rain keeps one from being bored," he said as they headed for the reference section. "Sunshine every day would be awful. Bor-ring, as Darcy would say."

Darcy grunted, then yawned. She seemed almost as out-of-sorts as Grandpop.

"What's the matter?" Brian asked her after the fourth yawn, as they were spreading B and V volumes of encyclopedias out on the reference table.

"I don't know," she said vaguely. "I kept hearing weird noises last night, from next door."

Numbles looked up, his finger marking a place. "Next door!" he exclaimed. "What next door? You've got a vacant lot on one side and an empty house on the other. What's to make noise?"

Darcy yawned again, and leaned her head on her hand, as if it were too heavy for her to hold up in the usual way. "I don't know," she said irritably. "All I know is that there were voices and thumps from the house, sort of like someone moving furniture or something."

"Any lights?" asked Brian, although he wasn't really paying attention. The bat pictures in front of him, especially the one of *Desmudus rotundus*, the common North American bat, looked a lot like the bats in Grandpop's barn. But nowhere could he find mention of one as large as the one they hadn't been able to catch.

"No," said Darcy, "no lights. At least not by the time I got up to look. And my mom said she was home all yesterday and no one was around. I was even wondering if someone was moving in. But at night . . ."

"No one moves in at night," said Numbles. "Hey, listen to this: 'Desmudontidae, the vampire bat . . .' "

"Yuck," said Darcy, leaning over his shoulder and peering at what he was reading.

"Tropical," said Numbles. "Three inches long with a wingspread of twelve inches."

"Not big enough," said Brian, disappointed, "for that last one."

"No," said Numbles, "but maybe okay for a couple of the others. Come on, listen: 'Goes to its victims' — get that, *victims* — 'on foot . . .' "

"Cows are too tall," said Darcy, yawning loudly.

" '. . . but jumps with great ease,' " Numbles read. "Here's the best part." He pushed the book to the middle of the table, and they all read:

Its narrow food passage allows only liquid to pass through. The vampire bat lives entirely on blood, hence its name. It usually consumes animal blood, especially cattle's, but has been known to bite humans. The wounds, made by biting out a small piece of skin, heal quickly. The bat does not suck, as the vampire of folklore is reputed to do, but instead laps the blood from the wounds. The bite itself is no more harmful than any bite, but vampire bats carry rabies and other diseases.

For a moment, they were all silent.

"Laps blood," said Brian softly. "That might explain the blood on the grass. Lapping's kind of messy. Especially if the bat bit into an artery. The wound would bleed pretty fast then. And I guess a vampire bat would lick any spilled blood off the cow's body, which would explain why there wasn't blood all over her hide."

"Mmm," said Numbles. "The trouble is," he went on, "that since the vet said there was no sign of disease, it has to be loss of blood that killed the cows—low blood volume, like he said. But could a vampire bat really eat enough of a cow's blood to kill it?"

"Over a period of days?" said Brian. "If it bit into an artery? Of course then it might die right away—"

"The calf," Darcy reminded them, "died quicker."

"That's right," said Brian. "She was smaller—she couldn't take as much blood loss." He banged his fist down on the table. "Blast it! I wish we'd looked at those bats more closely before we let them go!"

"We could go back and try to find them," Darcy suggested. She turned to VAMPIRE BAT in another encyclopedia and pointed to a picture accompanying the article. "I think Numbles is right that a couple of the ones we caught looked like these guys in the picture. A little, anyway."

"We'd have to know for sure," said Brian. "And it's too late now. Even if we did go back to the cave, we'd never find the right bats. And," he added, "this isn't the tropics; didn't that book say they're tropical?"

"Yeah," said Numbles. "Anyway, we'll know if they could have been vampire bats if the attacks stop. We won't have to worry about the one we left in the barn, though; he was too big."

"That bat in the barn is the wrong size for any kind of bat." Darcy pulled another volume toward her. "It says here that the biggest known bat has a five-foot wingspan. That might be okay, but it also says its body is the size of a pigeon's, which is definitely too small. That bat's body was huge! So I guess we're back to the poison and poisoner idea." Then she grinned and pointed to an entry just above VAMPIRE BAT in the encyclopedia Numbles had been reading.

VAMPIRE, it said.

"Maybe it's a real vampire." Darcy's grin broadened. "Not a vampire bat."

Numbles laughed, and Darcy made Dracula swooping motions and sucking noises until the librarian told her to stop.

But Brian walked away and looked out the window. Was that really such a crazy idea?

SHAPES IN THE NIGHT

THE RAIN STOPPED in late afternoon, but the air remained soggy and sultry. "We're in for a bad spell of heat," said Grandpop, reading the paper on the porch after supper. "Says here some kind of pressure system's worked its way east and north."

"Oh, dear." Grandmom fanned herself with a magazine. "And I was so hoping for a good night's sleep!"

By bedtime, Brian was also, but even with the window wide open and the covers pushed down to the foot of the bed, the room was stifling and he was miserable. He read for as long as he could, till his eyes burned and his mind couldn't concentrate even on "The Sign of Four," one of his favorite Holmes adventures. So he got up and, after turning off the light, leaned against the windowsill with Cadge panting softly beside him while he looked out over the darkened farm. There was no moon, but a faint star glow made shapes vaguely discernible—the barn, the near pasture fence,

Old Blue at the end of the driveway, Cadge stalking something near the far pasture fence . . .

Wait a minute. Cadge was right next to him!

Brian pressed his head against the screen. Then as quietly as possible he removed the screen and leaned out as far as he dared.

Something was indeed moving toward the far pasture, flowing along the ground, then up and over the fence—a large bird, perhaps? Yes, it looked like a bird, maybe a crow; there were plenty of big ones around.

Or an oversized bat. A huge one, in fact.

Much bigger than a vampire bat—

Brian felt his whole body stiffen. He was conscious of his own breathing as he watched, and of the beating of his heart.

"C'mon, Cadge," he said at last, knowing that if he hesitated any longer, he'd never move. He slipped his feet into his sneakers. "Let's go have a look."

He crept quietly down the stairs, with Cadge padding by his side—huddling close, as if he was nervous, too. Together they went out the front door, through the shadowy porch, and across the drive.

And there Cadge stopped, whimpering, his eyes on the dark field where the whatever-it-was had disappeared.

"What is it, boy?" Brian whispered, his hand on the dog's bristly neck.

Cadge turned and licked his hand, but when Brian moved forward, the dog wouldn't budge.

Shakier than ever now, Brian went on without him, but his heart thumped wildly in his chest and he could feel cold sweat chilling his back and sides, despite the breathless heat.

He stopped at the fence. There were no footprints that he could see. There was a scratch on one wooden fence post, but Brian had no idea if it had been there before or not. Blast it, he thought; Holmes would remember!

A slight motion at the far end of the field caught his eyes; a rustling sound, a low moo. But he couldn't see anything; would he have to go into the field?

Of course; how else would he find out what it was? And if it was what he feared . . .

He tried to make his mind's cloaked monster into a crazed man carrying an ancient South American blowgun, complete with arrow, its tip smeared with deadly curare.

But it didn't work; the monster image stayed.

Nonsense, he said to himself. Vampires aren't real.

He called softly to Cadge, but the dog only whimpered again, as if imploring Brian not to go farther. He's as nervous as he was around the dead cows, Brian realized; more so. There's got to be a connection.

Leaving Cadge, Brian walked to the gate, opened it, and went through. Then he paused; was that another rustle?

As his eyes got more used to the darkness, he thought he did see shapes in the far corner — two dark

shapes, one with lighter blotches—a cow, of course—
moving silently, as if wrestling—and something large
and black going up and down, floating, fluttering. I
should go over there, he told himself, but there seemed
to be something wrong with his feet, and for a moment he couldn't move.

By the time he could move, the shapes had separated and the blacker one had disappeared.

The other one—wasn't that it in the shadows, upright? So there was no need to go closer to it. Besides, whatever had happened had happened . . .

No, Brian, he thought, that's no good. You go over
there now; you find out what happened.

Then he nearly screamed, for he felt something
damp and cold against his hand. But it was only Cadge's
nose; the dog was no longer frightened, it seemed.

He went with Cadge across the field, tripping over
cow pats and rough ground, skirting cows—but most
of them were huddled in a corner away from where
the shapes had been—and then Cadge stopped, and
Brian stopped, too, only a few yards away from the
prone body of a cow. Cadge pulled away, and sat down,
panting.

It looked like a young cow this time—one of
Grandpop's year-old heifers.

Brian approached her cautiously—Cadge would go
no farther—and touched her neck. The heifer was dead
but still warm, and on his finger was a spot of sticky
wet blood.

"I decided to do an experiment," Grandpop said to the policeman who had come quickly in answer to his call. Brian had gone into the guest room, where Grandpop was sleeping, to wake him up; Grandpop had phoned the police right away. Now Brian, Grandpop, and the policeman were all out in the field with flashlights, standing around the body. "I put one sick cow alone in a field—she died the other day. I kept this one with the herd, and now she's dead, too. I've got one more sick one in the barn. We'll see what happens to her." He put his hand on Brian's shoulder. "At least this time Brian here saw someone go over the fence, like I said on the phone, and struggle with her. He found that wound in her neck, too. The county agent hasn't found any parasites or natural poisons. And now I'm convinced," he said grimly, "that my grandson was right all along, and someone *is* deliberately poisoning my cows, even if no one can find any evidence of it."

Brian turned away. It was ironic that Grandpop had accepted his theory just when he himself was beginning to doubt it.

Despondently, he excused himself and went back to the house.

Early that same morning Brian found Grandmom in the kitchen, listlessly making coffee; she'd obviously had another bad night. This time there were dark circles under her eyes, and her face looked pale above the scarf she'd tied around her neck.

Too upset even to speak to her, Brian went to the refrigerator and poured himself some milk. It was too bad about Grandmom, too bad that she was so tired—maybe even sick—just when all this was going on, too bad especially when she was always so nice to everyone else . . .

Wait a minute!

Hadn't Dad always said she'd do anything for Grandpop? *Anything?*

A glimmer of hope made Brian abandon his milk and leap up the stairs to his room, where he took down his complete Holmes, and flipped to the table of contents. Yes, there it was; why hadn't he thought of it before? "The Adventure of the Sussex Vampire."

Quickly, he found the story and skimmed through it, refreshing his memory: The usual distraught prospective client calls on Holmes, at his wits' end. This one suspects that his second wife is a bona fide Dracula-type vampire, and is gradually killing their baby. Holmes dismisses that idea as preposterous, since he is certain that vampires don't exist, but he agrees to take the case anyway.

I'm right, Brian thought excitedly, his mind and his memory clearing. This was the curare case! And . . .

He read on, eagerly.

Holmes and Watson are met at their client's house by the man's son by his first wife, a rather sappy teenager who dotes on his father. The second wife is by now very upset at her husband's accusation and will see no one. But the husband swears he has seen her rising from a bent-over position near the baby, lifting her head, with her mouth dripping blood. There is a wound in the baby's neck.

Brian skimmed down to Holmes's wonderfully re-assuring analysis: ". . . The idea of a vampire was to me absurd. Such things do not happen in criminal practice in England . . . Did it not occur to you that a bleeding wound may be sucked for some other pur-pose than to draw the blood from it? Was there not a queen in English history who sucked such a wound to draw poison from it?"

Holmes concluded that the poison was curare, or something similar, administered by the older boy out of jealousy of the baby. He didn't mention traceless-ness, at least not in that story. But who cares now, Brian thought, putting the book down and closing his eyes. Relief swept over him. There was no real vam-pire at all, preying on the cows as he'd feared for that wild moment in the library and again last night. There was a real person, just as he'd suspected, poisoning the cows, maybe with curare, maybe not; that no longer mattered much either. What mattered was Grand-mom. She must have gone into the field after the last couple of poisonings and tried to suck the poison out of the wound like the woman in the Holmes story.

It would be just like her.

Brian ran downstairs and back into the kitchen, where Grandmom was sitting at the table, her head in her hands as if exhausted. A bowl of half-beaten pancake batter was in front of her.

He touched her gently, and sat beside her. "Grandmom," he said softly. "Grandmom, it's all right. I know."

"What?" His grandmother raised her head and regarded him blankly. "Know what, dear?"

"What you've been trying to do for Grandpop's cows. But it's dangerous, Grandmom; you're making yourself sick. And last night's cow died anyway."

But Grandmom was staring at him as if he were crazy. "Brian, I don't have the slightest idea what you're talking about. Not the slightest."

"Oh, come on, Grandmom. It's a brave and wonderful thing, but . . ."

"Brian Larrabee," she said sternly, "I think you'd better tell me exactly what's on your mind before I think you've *lost* your mind!"

So he did, but he grew sickeningly less sure of himself as he progressed.

When he was finished, Grandmom hugged him and said, "Brian, dear, dear Brian, if there were prizes for imagination, you'd win them all, hands down. You're sweet to be so concerned about your grandfather's cows and his milk business, but better minds than ours are working on it, and I know they'll get to the bottom of it sooner or later. Meanwhile, the strain is getting to all of us. We need an excursion—an afternoon out, or maybe a night out. What do you say to a movie tonight? Maybe Numbles and Darcy could come, too." She pushed herself up from the table. "A nice wholesome movie," she said. "Not one of those awful horror things."

Darcy seemed even more preoccupied than Brian was himself during the movie, even though it was an exciting Western—her favorite kind of film next to sports stories, Numbles remarked when Brian had passed her the popcorn for the fourth time and she'd pushed it away.

The road was wet when they came out. There had been a thunderstorm, the popcorn seller said, quite a big one. "Maybe that'll cool things off," said Grandmom, loosening her scarf a little.

"Mmm," said Grandpop. "Just the idea of it getting cooler gives me an appetite. Let's go to the ice cream stand for a sundae."

Darcy was silent as they walked to Old Blue, and Brian couldn't help but noticing the strained expression on her face and the anxious way she kept looking behind her.

"What's the matter?" he asked when they got to the stand and the two of them got out of Old Blue and ordered the sundaes. "You sick or something?"

She shook her head.

"Well, you look awful."

"I didn't sleep last night." She faced him, and he was shocked to see fear in her eyes. "I tell you, Brian, something's going on in that house next door to me. My mom and I heard noises again last night, and she said she's going to call the cops if she hears them again."

"What kind of noises?" Brian asked cautiously.

"Not thumps so much this time. Voices. A kid arguing and someone shutting him up. And I saw . . ." She broke off as the girl behind the counter started pushing plastic dishes toward them.

"Two hot fudge," the girl said indifferently, "one butterscotch, a Coke, and a banana special with cherries, hot fudge, and blueberries." The Coke was for Grandmom, who still wasn't hungry. The special was for Numbles, and nearly turned Brian's stomach when he saw it.

"You don't understand," Darcy whispered, balancing the butterscotch between the two hot fudges when they'd paid and the girl had left. "It's not just the noises. Tonight? When I was walking to the corner to meet you guys? I could have sworn someone was staring at me out the window, from behind a curtain. But when I looked right at it, whoever it was pushed the curtain back into place and I couldn't see anything."

Brian carefully picked up the banana special in one hand and reached for the Coke with the other. The cream on one of the hot fudges that Darcy held was sliding down the mound of ice cream into the butter-scotch, but she didn't seem to notice. "Brian," she said, "don't you see? The poisoner! He could be using the empty house as his headquarters, and he could be staring out because he knows I'm helping to find out who he is!"

"Hey, you need a hand?" Numbles burst out of the darkness and reached eagerly for his banana special. "Oh, wow! Does that look good or does that look good?"

Darcy turned away, and Numbles followed, already spooning up his ice cream, but Brian felt his own footsteps lag and he wondered if Holmes had ever felt as reluctant as he to go on pursuing a case when the real truth finally began to emerge.

Headquarters, he was thinking. Using the house next door to Darcy's as headquarters . . .

WHATEVER REMAINS

THE LARRABEES' PHONE RANG the next morning before Brian was fully awake, jolting him out of a half-dream in which Sherlock Holmes and Watson tracked a giant iguana—there had been one in last night's movie—into a deserted house where a gang of long-toothed robbers in capes and ten-gallon hats were counting their loot.

"Brian!" came Grandpop's voice up the stairs. "It's Darcy. You awake?"

"I am now," Brian grumbled, swinging his feet to the floor and rubbing his eyes. "I'll take it on the extension up here."

His grandfather appeared in the doorway. "I'd rather you didn't," he said. "Your grandmother didn't sleep well again last night."

Grandmom!

Brian closed his eyes for a moment, seeing Grandmom's pale face, her tired eyes—and the scarf around her neck. Why would she have been wearing a scarf on a hot and humid day? She'd even worn it last night, hadn't she, when it was hotter still? Of course, if she was sick, she could have been having a chill—

He opened his eyes and forced himself to look calmly at Grandpop. "Okay," he said. "Tell Darcy I'll be right there."

Or, he said to himself as Grandpop nodded and left, Grandmom could have been hiding something—a small, two-pronged wound?

Shuddering, Brian skinned off his pajamas and dressed quickly in shorts and an old T-shirt; he could already feel that the day was going to be another scorcher. Would Grandmom wear her scarf again to-day?

Brian ran downstairs to the phone and said "Hi, Darce" with forced cheerfulness. "What's up?"

"Brian, I have to see you right away," Darcy said urgently. "Can you come over? I'm calling Numbles, too. Something terrible is going on, I know it. I—I was followed last night . . ."

Brian's heart sank, but aloud he said briskly, "Oh, come on, how could you have been? We dropped you off right at your front door."

"Yes, I know, but I went out again. I left my bike out, and Mom said it might rain again, which of course it did. I went to put my bike away, and then I remem-bered I'd borrowed a softball from James Bantry who lives down the street, so I thought I'd take it over and put it on his porch. And—I'll tell you when I see you," she added hastily, and hung up.

Breakfast, Brian reminded himself, going to the kitchen. Breakfast first. And Grandmom.

But Grandmom still hadn't come downstairs. Brian took out the cornflakes, trying to concentrate on the light rustling sound they made when he poured them into the bowl. Like dry leaves, he thought, or sand . . .

"Oh, good." It was Grandpop, coming in, a mug of coffee in his hand. "I see you're fending for yourself. Want some berries on it? There's some blueberries in the fridge."

"No thanks." Numbles's banana special rose unpleasantly before his eyes at the mention of blueberries. "I'm not very hungry."

"Seems like I'm the only one who is any more," said Grandpop. "Your grandmother didn't eat a thing except a little beef broth that she asked me to take up to her. Strange kind of thing to want for breakfast, if you ask me."

"How's she feeling?" Brian asked, trying to sound casual. "She still in bed?"

Grandpop nodded. "She had bad dreams again. Said she heard noises, too. A sort of flapping, like a bird flying around. You hear anything? She said to ask you, since your room's on the same side as hers. Said she thought there was a hawk or something trying to get in. Doesn't make sense, though. Hawks don't fly at night."

Brian felt himself start to sweat. "Nighthawks?" he suggested without conviction. "Owls?"

"Umm. Could be. All this lack of sleep," said Grandpop, "it's not good for the mind. You get your own lunch today, okay? I told your grandmother to stay in bed awhile. I'll have her to the doctor tomorrow if she's no better. Maybe he can give her some pills."

"I'm going to the village," Brian said. "Darcy wants me to come over." And, he said to himself, I want to go back to that library.

"Chores first," reminded Grandpop. "Don't forget that sick cow in the barn. At least she's still alive. Maybe the dang poisoner won't go in there."

Brian nodded—but he was almost certain Grandpop would be proved wrong.

Cadge followed him to the barn but stayed outside when he went in. There wasn't much mucking out to do with just one cow inside. She was listless and weak, and turned her sad brown eyes on Brian as he moved around her. "Poor Bossy," he said, stroking her, feeling along her neck. Sure enough, he found a rough spot, and when he probed under the hair there were two small openings just as he'd feared, with what looked like dried blood around the edges.

Brian sat down heavily on a hay bale. Somehow this clinched it; there could be no other explanation.

Could there?

Holmes would laugh.

But Brian knew he couldn't tell himself any more that there were no such things as vampires, as Holmes had when that man in Sussex thought his wife was one. After all, Brian reasoned, there have been vampire legends all over the world, century after century. Maybe they aren't just legends. Why would they be so common, so persistent and widespread, if there were no truth in them?

I have to find out, he said to himself, if anyone's ever proved scientifically that vampires *don't* exist.

What was it that Holmes used to say? "When you have excluded the impossible, whatever remains, however improbable, must be the truth"?

Poisoning seems impossible now, Brian thought.

And nothing I can think of—except a vampire—makes this kind of wound and causes this kind of sickness.

So wouldn't even Holmes agree it's got to be a vampire? Even though that's improbable? Holmes or no Holmes, it seems *possible*, given all the legends.

Maybe Holmes wasn't aware of them.

His head spinning, Brian finished his chores, washing out the old-fashioned metal milk cans whose contents he knew Grandpop had dumped out earlier, in private. He never wanted anyone with him when he did that, for he said it nearly made him cry each time. And no wonder, Brian thought, scrubbing the last can and forcing his mind to change direction; with no milk being sold, there can't be any money coming in. Grandmom had brought only two bags of groceries home the other day instead of her usual four. Maybe I can get myself invited to Numbles's or Darcy's for dinner a few times. That might make things a little easier for Grandmom and Grandpop.

Or better yet, maybe I can figure out what's really going on.

Heat had already softened the road to the village even though it was still fairly early when Brian set out on Grandpop's old bike. Cicadas hummed in the distance, making the day seem hotter, and the exhaust smells from the few cars that passed lay heavily in the air.

By the time Brian got to Darcy's street, his face was pouring sweat and his shirt was sticking to his back. He took it off, dried himself with it, and draped it over the handlebars.

Darcy was waiting on her front porch, looking cool but worried.

"So," he said, feigning cheerfulness as he loped up the steps and sat on the railing, facing her. "What's all this about being followed?"

"As soon as I left the yard," she said, almost whispering, "I heard something behind me. Like footsteps. So I did the thing they always do on TV and in the movies. I stopped, and it stopped. I speeded up and it speeded up. I kept turning around to see if I could see anything, but I couldn't. It was kind of foggy anyway; you know, misty."

Brian frowned. "Foggy? It wasn't foggy out at our place. Anyway, not that I noticed."

"Well, it was here," said Darcy, "at least once I was out walking. I don't remember that it was when you guys dropped me off."

"Neither do I." Brian paused, thinking. "How long was it between the time we dropped you off and the time you went out again?"

"Only a couple of seconds."

"And it was foggy right away?"

"No. Not until I turned around the first time to see who was following me. It was like the fog was behind me."

"And not in front?"

She shrugged. "I know that sounds weird, but that's how it was. I didn't think much of it at the time. I was too scared. But, yeah, you're right. That is weird."

"Did you see the fog again when you went back to your house? I mean, did you go through it on the way back?"

"No, I don't think so. But I ran back, Brian, so I don't know. A lot later there were noises next door again, and my parents called the police, and they came. I watched out the window, only it was still pretty dark. They broke in, and Dad told me they said they didn't find anyone. But then after they'd been gone a while,

I heard the noises again. Voices—you know. A kid's voice, like before, and someone shushing it."

Brian got off the railing and began to pace.

"I called Numbles. He thinks we should have a look at the house ourselves. So do I. He's coming over."

Fog, thought Brian. Isn't there something about vampires and fog?

But why Darcy? Okay, so she's trying to help find the killer, but still, I'm the main one looking. And— he felt an unpleasant chill—nothing's come after me yet.

But then there's Grandmom.

"Hi, Bri, Darcy." Numbles puffed along the sidewalk and up Darcy's front walk. "I got here as soon as I could."

"Hi, Numbles," said Darcy.

Brian just nodded, his mind still working.

Maybe the—the suspect—is really after Grandmom, and the cows are just a distraction.

Or—here Brian hit his palm with his fist—or he's after Grandpop and he's trying to get at him through her *and* through the cows!

"Hey, Bri," said Numbles. "You okay?"

"Revenge," whispered Brian, hardly aware he'd spoken out loud. "We're back to that. It's got to be revenge."

"What does, Holmes?"

"Huh?"

"Brian, are you with us?" asked Darcy.

"Yes, sorry. I was just thinking. What?"

"These great minds," said Numbles to Darcy. "There's no telling when they're going to start working overtime." He poked Brian's arm. "Come on, Holmes," he said. "Let's go look at this house of Inspector Lestrade's."

"Huh?" said Brian. "Oh, you mean the one Darcy's suspicious of. Yes. Okay. Let's go." And then hit the encyclopedias, he said to himself. Read *Dracula*, too, maybe. There's a book, isn't there, as well as the movie? He'd seen the movie a couple of years ago.

They crossed Darcy's side lawn in silence and stood looking up at the house. It was a large three-story one, with dusty empty windows and peeling paint. A wide porch sagged across its front, with two or three floorboards missing.

"Maybe we should wait till night," Numbles said uncertainly. "When we can't be seen."

"No," Darcy said. "Not on your life. That'd give them more time to do whatever it is they're doing." She started up the front steps, which creaked and bent under her weight. "One at a time on each step," she whispered, "or I bet we'll fall through."

A curtain hung over the window in the front door, so there was no way to look inside.

Brian tried the door. Locked.

So were the windows that gave out onto the porch, and the drapes were tightly closed on all but one.

Brian put his face to the glass of that window, shielding it from sunlight with his hands.

At first it was too dark inside to make anything out.

Then he saw several large pieces of furniture—a sofa, probably; a couple of armchairs; a coffee table. All of them were neatly covered with some kind of white material—dust covers, Grandmom would probably call them. Several other large low pieces of furniture were arranged at the left side of the room, under the windows there. They didn't seem to be covered, but he couldn't tell what they were. Benches, maybe? Window seats?

"Do you see those chests?" whispered Numbles, leaning against Brian's shoulder.

"You mean those low things?" Brian asked, looking again. "Yes, I suppose they could be chests. Like the kind people keep blankets in. Funny things to have in a living room, though." Not so funny, he said to himself, if . . .

"Maybe they're not chests," said Darcy, pushing Numbles aside and looking herself. "Maybe they're, you know, crates of some kind. Packing crates. They look sort of box-like."

"They'd sure hold a lot of curare," Numbles said slowly. "Or a lot of blowguns."

Brian didn't dispute him. But scenes from the movie *Dracula* popped uncomfortably into his mind—vampires lying in coffins, in big wooden boxes of earth . . .

Quietly, he went around to the left-hand side of the house, which was the side away from Darcy's. But there was no way to reach the windows there in order to look in.

"If anyone's here right now," said Numbles, joining him with Darcy, "they sure are being quiet."

"Come back in about twelve hours," said Darcy, as they continued on to the back, "and you'll see. Good grief, look at all this!"

Brian followed Darcy's pointing finger and saw a trail of thick clods of muddy earth, as if they'd fallen off someone's shoes after a heavy rainstorm, leading from the back door to the stone wall at the far end of the back yard.

"What's behind the wall?" asked Brian, bending to examine one of the clods. "No, Numbles, don't touch them! They're evidence."

"There's nothing much behind the wall," said Darcy. "Just a—oh, wow!"

"Whoops," said Numbles.

"Oh, wow, what?" asked Brian. "Whoops, what?"

Darcy and Numbles were staring at each other, their mouths twitching. Then they both guffawed simultaneously.

"It's just that the only thing back there is a cemetery," Numbles explained.

"Yeah," said Darcy, "and Numbles and I must've had the same thought at the same time—ghosts!" She laughed again. "Can't you just see it? This tall guy in a sheet . . ."

"Winding sheet," said Numbles, "like the covers on that furniture . . ."

"Right. Hopping out of his grave, messing up the dirt, and climbing over the wall to—to . . ."

"To haunt the house next door to you, Darce, with his screaming ghost-kid. Oh, that's rich!"

Brian straightened up and walked to the wall. *"Whatever remains, no matter how improbable . . ."*

"There may be more to this than you think," he said soberly to the others. "Let's have a look in that graveyard."

"Oh, come on, Brian, you don't . . ."

Brian shrugged. "Call it a hunch, Numbles," he said. "Come on. Let's have a look anyway. Can't hurt." In his mind, though, he was ticking off the evidence once more: loss of blood volume; Grandmom weak, wearing a scarf on a hot day and having bad dreams—at least thinking they were dreams; weren't bad dreams in the Dracula movie really vampire attacks?—mist going after Darcy; the huge bat—vampires can turn into bats, can't they, as well as mist?—packing crates in the house next door; a handy cemetery . . .

Maybe I don't even have to do any research.

Brian followed Numbles over the wall; Darcy was already quite far ahead. The dirt clods led along a rough path, lined with tombstones, some upright, others flush with the ground. There were one or two marble buildings with angels and vines carved on them, and a wheelbarrow with sod and a shovel in it, as if someone had just dug a grave.

"Creepy, huh?" said Numbles as they passed beneath the cold stare of a formidable statue—a woman with a sword in one hand and a book in the other. "Wonder who she's supposed to be."

" 'The Angel of Death,' " Brian read from the statue's base. "Whew!"

"Looks more like a devil," said Numbles. "What a face!"

"Brian! Numbles!" called Darcy from what seemed like the other end of the graveyard. She had been laughing when she'd climbed over the stone wall, but now she sounded tense and a little frightened. "Come here."

They followed her voice and the dirt clods to three graves clustered together in an out-of-the-way corner of the cemetery. "Those bunches of dirt lead right here," Darcy said in a hushed voice. "And look . . ."

There was fresh dirt around all three graves, as if they'd recently been disturbed. GEORGE KNOWLES was carved on the largest stone marker, and the date was May 18 of the spring just past.

CHRISTINA KNOWLES was the inscription on the next-largest stone, and a small one between the two read: GEORGE KNOWLES, JUNIOR. The dates on the other two were within weeks of the date on the first.

Brian rubbed his forehead. Knowles. Wasn't that the name of that farmhand Grandpop had fired? Revenge . . .

Shakily, Brian sat down on a nearby rock. He was sure now—but how was he ever going to convince the others?

NOT QUITE GHOSTS

ALL BRIAN SAID to Numbles and Darcy, before biking back to the farm for lunch, was that he had a new theory and wanted to test it before he told them about it. Holmes, after all, often kept his ideas from Watson till he was really sure of them.

I *do* still have to check out Grandmom, Brian thought, pulling into Grandpop's driveway and parking his bike by the porch. And find out more about that Knowles guy.

As soon as he walked into the kitchen, he saw that Grandmom was still wearing her scarf. "Feeling better?" he asked casually, standing next to her at the sink to wash his hands.

"A little. You have a nice bike ride?"

"Okay—hot, though." He reached for a hand towel. Maybe that was the way to approach it—the heat. "Grandmom," he said, "aren't you awfully hot in that scarf?"

She laughed nervously and pulled at it a little. "Yes, I suppose I am," she said. "But I—oh, it's just foolish vanity, Brian; I'm a silly old woman! It's nothing, only I have a queer bug bite on my neck, and—well, your grandfather worries so, I didn't want him to see it."

"Queer?" asked Brian carefully. "What do you mean?"

"Ugly, really, instead of queer. Biggish."

"Maybe you should see a doctor, if it's a lump or something, I mean."

"Oh, hush, dear, you're as bad as your grandfather! And anyway"—she patted his cheek—"it bleeds some; it's more of a wound than a lump. I'd take the scarf off and just wear the BandAid I've got on, but your grandfather'd notice that." She chuckled. "It used to bother me that he never seemed to see what I was wearing, but I'm glad of it now. Now come on, we can't stand here chattering. Your grandfather will be looking for his lunch any minute. Just get me the bread, would you? There's a dear!"

Grandpop grumbled so much at lunch about the heat and the sudden thunderstorms and his money troubles that Brian didn't get a chance to ask him about George Knowles. But after lunch, when Grandpop went out to the vegetable garden to pick a head of lettuce Grandmom had asked for, he did have a chance to ask Grandmom about her bad dreams—what she thought were dreams, anyway.

"Oh, my," she answered. "I don't know as I want to talk about them. They're rather awful and rather— inappropriate for young ears." She tweaked his nose. "Another time, dear, okay?"

Grandpop came in from the garden then and put the lettuce down on the counter. "Here you are, Jessie, though I must say I wish you'd eat some of it yourself instead of just making salads out of it for us." He turned gloomily back to the door.

"Grandpop," said Brian quickly, before he could get away, "could you tell me again about that farmhand you had? Knowles, wasn't it?"

"Yep," Grandpop said gruffly. "Nothing much to tell. He was a lazy son-of-a-gun, like I said, and he died last spring, like I said, too. His wife and son died soon after that, I heard, which made me feel sorry. Some wasting disease got all of 'em; must've been contagious."

"It was very sad," said Grandmom. "I always felt sorry for them myself, but there was nothing your grandfather could do."

"I wondered after George Knowles died if that disease was what made him so lazy," said Grandpop. "Wish he'd told me he was sick. I'd have paid for a doctor, right enough. I even suggested it, but he wouldn't go. Wish I'd made him. But it's too late for that kind of regret now."

"You said they died in the spring?" asked Brian. He realized he was twisting the dish towel; he shook it out and hung it up.

"May, I think," Grandpop answered. "Least that was when George died. I remember the funerals. Went to George's, but not to the others."

"The funerals. Were they here in Oak Grove?"

"Yep, right here. Always struck me as odd, because I didn't think the family was from here originally. But, yes, right here. All three of 'em, and they were all buried right here, too. What're you so curious about all that for?"

"Oh, I saw some graves marked Knowles in the village cemetery today. I just wondered if it was them."

"Must be. It's not a common name around here." Grandpop went to the back door. "If you've got nothing to do, Bri, you could help me and Cadge move the heifers to the far pasture. 'Course if you've got plans . . ."

"No, no," said Brian. "That'd be fine."

For the better part of the afternoon, Brian helped his grandfather and Cadge move the heifers, and by the time they were finished, it was milking time, and after they'd finished with that, Brian offered to dump the milk, to spare Grandpop for once.

Grandpop agreed, and even let him drive the tractor by himself to the dumping spot.

Brian kept his mind as blank as possible while he watched the white milk seep into the soft brown earth. Grandpop had dug a series of shallow pits in one corner of an unused field, so he could rotate dumping spots.

Flies buzzed above the soggy ground; the sky overhead was a hazy blue with towering white clouds. It was hard to believe that anything so ancient, so evil as a vampire could exist under such a sky.

Well, of course it can't, Brian thought. If that Dracula movie is accurate, vampires can't be outside during the day.

I've got to sleep in the barn tonight, with that sick cow. There's no way out of it. I've got to, just to make sure.

The weather turned more sultry that evening, and it didn't get any cooler after a suppertime thunderstorm. By the time Brian's grandparents were in bed and Brian had crept stealthily outside, it was hotter in the barn than anywhere else. Hay prickled into Brian's back as he tossed around on the bales he'd made into a bed; Cadge, who gave the sick cow a wide berth, curled up in an uneasy ball near the door.

It was eleven-thirty, and already Brian felt sleepy. Maybe he could catch a few winks; he planned to set his alarm watch to go off every hour so he could check on the cow regularly. It would be better, he thought, if Numbles and Darcy were here, too. Then we could sleep in shifts, and keep watch every minute.

But of course they don't even know yet what we're looking for.

A few hours later, not long before his watch was due to go off for the fourth time, Brian sat bolt upright, at first not sure where he was or what had awakened him. Then he saw Cadge huddled against the closed door, trembling. He looked too terrified to growl.

Brian followed the dog's eyes and then froze. Above him, climbing into the loft window, was the large bat they'd been unable to clear out of the barn — climbing *in*, not out.

That proves, Brian said to himself, staring, that it probably doesn't live here as we thought when we first saw it.

And if that's true, it could live in one of those packing crates next door to Darcy's, the way Dracula lived or at least slept in a wooden box during the day in the movie.

Brian stayed very still, hardly daring to breathe. Would the creature attack him? Could it really be George Knowles? It seemed impossible — but maybe, as Holmes would say, it was only improbable.

The bat shook itself, its huge wings casting their shadow over Brian in the moonlight. Brian looked away when the beady red eyes found his and held them for a moment.

When he looked back, the bat was gone, and in its place was a thin mist that curled upward and floated lazily out the window.

Brian rubbed his eyes. The sick cow was standing serenely in her stall — but . . .

"Oh, good grief!" Brian said aloud. "Grandmom!"

He bolted out of the barn and into the house.

The door to her room was closed, as it had been, Brian realized, for the last several nights. He wrenched it open, looked fearfully toward the bed—and realized he was too late. Knowles must have attacked her before going to the barn.

Grandmom lay there, sound asleep in the moonlight, her lips curled back in an odd half smile, a smile that seemed somehow tinged with evil. Was it his imagination, or— He approached the bed and saw to his horror that her canine teeth had grown, although not so much that one would notice unless one looked closely. But—Brian tried to remember—wasn't that supposed to happen to people as they gradually became vampires as a result of vampire attacks?

The scarf was on the table beside the bed, and on the soft white skin of Grandmom's throat, on one side, were two ragged punctures. There was a spot of blood on her pillow.

Briefly, Brian felt sick. Then he saw the window— wide open. Its old-fashioned wood-frame screen fit so loosely there was about a sixteenth of an inch of space between it and the windowsill.

Trying not to shake, Brian crossed the room and examined the space more closely, thinking he should stuff it with something as soon as Grandmom got up.

But what good will that do, he thought, against a creature that can turn to mist and might even be able to filter itself through the screen's mesh?

I've got to tell the others, he said to himself; even if they laugh at the idea, I've got to tell them. No adult's going to believe this, especially not Grandpop. And I need help—fast.

The next morning, Grandmom stayed in bed again. "She hardly spoke to me when I went in to see how she was," Grandpop told Brian. "She just kept moaning and saying what sounded like 'Knowles, Knowles.' But that's crazy. She never even liked the man."

Brian tried to sound calm. "Maybe she dreamed about him."

"Maybe. But I'm calling the doctor anyway." Grandpop reached for the phone. It rang, though, before he could pick it up, and he grabbed the receiver out of its cradle and barked, "Yes?" angrily into it.

"It's Numbles," he said a second later, holding the receiver out to Brian. "Make it snappy, okay?"

Brian nodded and put the phone to his ear. "Hi," he said.

"Brian," said Numbles, his voice sounding oddly shaken. "Something's happened. You'd better come right over, okay?"

Brian's mouth went dry. "Okay. Sure. Is Darcy all right?"

"Yeah, fine. She's here with me. We're both a little—well, you'll see. You will be, too, when you know."

"I'll be over as soon as I can. Right after chores."

Brian put the receiver down, said "Good luck with

the doctor" to his grandfather, and left hastily for the barn.

Numbles and Darcy were on the porch outside Numbles's collecting room when Brian rode up on Grandpop's old bike. Both of them were ashen; Numbles looked dangerously close to tears. "Tex is gone," he said. "Just—vanished. Not escaped; there's no sign he forced his way out. And he wouldn't do that anyway. He likes me . . ."

Brian put his hand on Numbles's shoulder. "Steady," he said softly.

"Brian, you have to see outside his cage," said Darcy. "There's blood all over the place, like he got hurt fighting whatever it was, or like—like he was murdered."

"No." Numbles's voice was choked. "I told you, that's not it. Probably not, anyway. Horned lizards have this weird thing. They shoot blood from their eyes sometimes. Like—like when they're scared—I'm not sure. As far as I know, Tex has never done it, but he must've this time, because, look."

He showed Brian two spots of blood on the wall opposite the cage, with spatter marks around them, as if the blood had been shot from a water pistol.

Darcy shook her head. "I hope you're right," she said darkly. "But I still think . . ."

"I left Tex out here on the porch last night," Numbles interrupted, "because it was so hot. I thought he'd like it. And now . . ."

Brian gave Numbles another pat on the shoulder and went down the porch steps, pacing around the yard. Rosey was still there; her pen looked undisturbed

"Nothing else is missing, right?" he called back to Numbles.

"Nothing."

"And, Darcy, did you hear your noises last night?"

"Yes. The same kid—everything. Maybe a little louder."

Brian walked back to them. "Okay," he said. "Sit down. I've got a theory. And I think it's more than a theory, I think it's the truth. I know you're going to laugh at me . . ."

". . . No," said Numbles softly when Brian had finished. "No, I'm not going to laugh at you."

But Darcy looked as if she couldn't believe her ears. "Come on, Bri," she said. "I wasn't serious when I said that about vampires. There's no such thing . . ."

"You can't study reptiles," said Numbles, giving her a withering look, "without realizing that there are—and were—a lot of strange creatures in the world. Do you know they've recently found fish that people once thought had been extinct for millions of years? Some reptiles—well, they're a lot like the monsters you read about. There's a theory that dragons might have been leftover dinosaurs, for instance, hidden away—the last survivors of their species. As a scientist, I have to believe that anything is possible; I can't rule anything out. And so I can't rule out your theory, Brian. Especially after what you said about your grandmother. I mean, any *real* criminal would just have murdered her, right?"

Brian felt an odd prickling sensation at the back of his neck. "Probably," he said. "Yes."

"Sheesh," said Darcy.

"If something scared Tex," said Brian, "he'd shoot his blood out, right?"

"I think so."

"So," said Brian, "if an intruder came up on your porch, maybe looking to break into your house, and Tex got scared, he'd shoot his blood. And if that intruder were a vampire . . ."

"The vampire mightn't be able to resist the blood, so he'd grab Tex," said Numbles. "But then . . ." His eyes filled. "Then Tex is probably dead."

"Not necessarily." Darcy put her hand on his. "He's got awfully thick skin. But, Brian . . ."

"It's the one thing that fits all the evidence, Darcy. For everything, I mean. Creatures attacked by vampires get progressively weaker, like the cows, and like my grandmother, at least that's what happens in the movie of *Dracula*. They have wounds in the neck."

"Not all of your grandfather's cows did get progressively weaker," said Darcy stubbornly. "What about the calf?"

"She was small," Brian said promptly. "It wouldn't have taken long to get enough blood from her to kill her."

"Vampires can turn into fog, Darcy," said Numbles softly. "And bats. That's in all the movies, and besides, I read it, too, a couple of years ago. When I first heard that theory about dragons and dinosaurs, I did a lot of reading about vampires and other things like that." He looked thoughtful. "Most legends say that in the daytime vampires have to lie in their native soil or in the soil they were buried in, in coffins or some kind of box like a coffin. The sun kills them, supposedly—I mean destroys them. They're already dead, sort of. 'Undead,' I think is the term."

"Sheesh," said Darcy. "Undead—that's creepy. Hey!" She brightened. "Those packing crates in the empty house. They could be vampire beds."

"Right," said Brian.

"And that means there's more than one vampire," said Numbles.

"Yeah," Darcy agreed. "And the disturbed graves, too. There were a couple of them."

"Three," Brian reminded them. "Remember I said George Knowles, that farmhand my grandfather fired, had a wife and a kid."

"Sheesh," said Darcy again. "You sure are right that it all fits."

"Motive and everything," said Numbles.

"The kid I heard!" Darcy exclaimed. "That must've been the vampire kid. Of course they were trying to shush him! And remember the fat little bat in the cave? That could've been him, too. I wonder how he got back to the house, though."

"Darcy," said Brian, "didn't you hear those moving-in noises right after we cleared out the barn?"

"Yes."

"Of course!" said Numbles. "They moved into the house so they wouldn't have to risk being cleared out of the barn again."

"So instead of being poison hunters like we thought," said Darcy, "I guess we have to be monster hunters. We've sure got to save Mrs. Larrabee."

"Monster hunters it is," said Numbles.

"Thank you," Brian said huskily, around the sudden lump in his throat.

Darcy got up and went to the edge of the porch. "Well, come on," she said. "We better check out those packing crates or coffins or whatever they are. Let's go nab the vampires while they're sleeping. Run them through with stakes, pow, right in the heart. Isn't that what they did to Dracula? Let's go! Maybe we'll even be in time to save Tex."

DARCY IN DANGER

"HOLD ON, DARCY," said Brian. "Let's think this through. We need a foolproof plan."

"Yeah," said Numbles. "Much as I want to save Tex"—he blew his nose—"I don't want to end up a vampire myself. That's what happens if they fix you with their eyes while you're trying to stake them, I think. Or even just look at you."

"Oh, yeah?" said Darcy. "How come you know so much about it?"

"I told you, I read about them a couple of years ago." Numbles turned to Brian. "Maybe we should at least be *ready* to stake them, though. You do know, don't you, that a person who dies as a result of vampire attacks becomes a vampire after death?"

"Yeah," said Brian. "At least I'm pretty sure. That's what happens in *Dracula*, anyway." He thought it through for a minute. The idea of spearing a corpse didn't appeal to him much. But if it was to save

Grandmom, and the farm . . . "Okay, but just *ready* to stake," he told them. "We better not actually do it unless we really have to."

According to Numbles, the best staking material was ash or whitethorn. Failing that, oak. They finally found an oak tree among the maples in Numbles's yard, and Darcy volunteered to climb up and cut three good branches.

They spent the rest of the morning peeling the bark off and sharpening their stakes.

"They have to be staked in the daytime, don't they?" asked Darcy when they were about to split up for lunch.

"I guess," said Numbles. "At least that's when they're at home and powerless, except maybe for those staring eyes. But don't you try anything, Darce," he warned. "Hand over that stake."

"No way," said Darcy, seizing her stake and ramming it into the ground. "Bam!" she cried. "Take that for Mrs. Larrabee." She pulled the stake out and jammed it in again. "And that for Mr. Larrabee's cows."

"Darcy," Numbles said wearily, grabbing the stake from her. "Go home. Have a nice lunch. We'll see you later."

"I think," said Brian, watching Darcy bike angrily down the street, "that you and I better work out a plan."

"I've got a meeting of the Herpetologist Society this afternoon," Numbles said apologetically. "Field trip, actually."

"Can you skip it?"

"I'm afraid not. I have to help lead."

"Think of Tex." And of my grandmother, Brian added silently.

"I am thinking of Tex, believe me. But he'd want me to go."

Brian gave Numbles a look, but he seemed perfectly serious. "We've got to act pretty fast," he said. "I don't think Grandmom's got much time."

Numbles put his hand on Brian's arm. "Yeah, I know," he said quietly. "Tell you what. Ask if you can sleep over tonight. We can plan then. But maybe first you should put garlic around your grandmother's door and window. I remember reading that now—vampires hate garlic."

"Wasn't it something else in the Dracula movie?" Brian asked skeptically. "Crosses, I think. And some other kind of plant—not garlic. Wolf's-something?"

"I never saw that movie," Numbles said. "But, hey, movies change things." He thought a minute. "Maybe it was wolfsbane; I think I've read about that, too. But take it from me, Bri, garlic's in a lot of books. And it ought to be pretty easy to get hold of." Numbles's face suddenly grew very serious. "You're right about our needing a foolproof plan," he said. "If we *do* stake them, we've got to make very, very sure we get them the first time." He hefted one of the stakes dubiously. "I'm not sure I could do it. Plunge this into someone's chest. Even if the someone were dead. Undead. Whatever."

"I'm not either," Brian admitted. "Darcy's probably the only one of us who could."

Numbles said "Ha!" scornfully, but Brian felt sure he agreed nonetheless.

It was a slow, hot afternoon, with the usual threat of a thunderstorm at the end of the day or during the night. Brian went back to the farm for lunch, and found Grandmom even paler than before, slowly doing dishes. He decided to follow Numbles's advice about the garlic, but later, to make sure it would be fresh. Since Grandmom was in the kitchen, he couldn't check her garlic supply, but when he went back to the village he bought two bottles of garlic juice, figuring whole garlic or garlic powder would be too noticeable anyway. Then he went to the cemetery and stared down at the Knowleses' untidy graves.

We're assuming they're in the house, he thought, but we haven't actually seen them there. They could be here instead, lying underground on their backs with their eyes staring and their long teeth ready to grab us . . .

He felt goosebumps in spite of the heat.

I've got to know, he said to himself. I've got to be sure where they are if we're going to stake them. And I'd rather check the house than dig up their graves.

He turned and followed the strewn-dirt path through the graveyard, past the Angel of Death statue, and over the wall to the deserted house. For a moment he paused, trying to control the shaking his body seemed determined to do. Holmes always seemed calm, he said to himself; I wonder what he felt like inside, though. Maybe terrified. Maybe he just hid it well.

Steadied by that thought, Brian crept up the back steps and tried the door.

It opened easily. A dim glow coming through a window showed him he was in the kitchen. Cobwebs brushed his hand as he reached for a light, and nothing happened when he flipped the switch. But what he could see of the kitchen looked normal enough — just dusty. Neat, too. There were no dirty dishes around, no signs of food.

Figures. Vampires don't eat food.

He opened the refrigerator, half expecting to see bottles of blood, as in a hospital. But it was dark inside and there was nothing there.

The next room was the dining room; six chairs, draped with dust covers, ringed a large table, like executives at a meeting. Fancy china was displayed in a corner cupboard, and there was a fireplace with brass andirons at one end of the room.

An archway led into the living room, and here Brian paused, his eyes drawn immediately to the two large wooden crates and one smaller one that stood under the side windows.

He couldn't stop now, at least his feet wouldn't; they led him straight under the arch and into the room.

The three crates were open. The largest one's lid was leaning neatly against the wall, and the lids of the other two were pushed back partway, almost as if they were serving as blankets. A small white square was fastened to the middle-sized crate's blanket-lid.

The white square was a scrap of paper, with a note written on it in dull brownish red letters—blood, Brian realized.

STAYING IN BARN TODAY. ALMOST THROUGH.
BACK AFTER DARK, TWICE MORE SHOULD DO IT.
MAYBE THREE TIMES. AND THEN THE BOY.

The inside of Brian's mouth turned to sandpaper. *And then the boy.*

There was no doubt in his mind that the *barn* was his grandfather's, that *twice more* and *maybe three times* referred to Grandmom, and that *the boy* meant himself.

It was a good thing Numbles had remembered about garlic.

Unconsciously, Brian put his hand to his throat. Then he looked inside the crates.

The largest one was empty, but the middle-sized one wasn't. There, on a bed of neatly raked earth, lay a woman, apparently sleeping, but with her eyes wide open. Brian stepped back into the shadows quickly. The woman's face was deathly pale except for two spots of red, like a fever blush, that showed high on her cheekbones. Her lips were red and cruel, and protruding under the top one were her two canine teeth, unnaturally long and as pointed as daggers.

For a moment, Brian thought he was going to pass

out. His head spun dizzily and he reeled back, bumping into the smaller crate and then recoiling, spinning
away from what lay there—a small plump boy, with
the same red fever blush, the same protruding teeth—
and for some reason, a look of terror in his open eyes.

Can he know, Brian thought wildly, what we're
probably going to do to him?

He ran blindly from the room, bumping into furniture and nearly falling down the back steps on his
way out. Gasping, he leaped over the hedge that separated the "empty" house from Darcy's and up onto
her porch, where he leaned on the doorbell.

"Is—Darcy—home?" he managed to blurt out to
Mrs. Verona, who looked at him with concern and
shook her head.

"No, dear, I haven't seen her since lunch. She must
be at practice now. Are you all right?"

Brian nodded and managed to say, "Tell her—to
sit tight. Not to do anything till she hears from me.
I'll try to catch her."

And he was off down the street, running toward the
ball field, while Mrs. Verona looked anxiously after
him.

But Darcy wasn't at practice, one of the other kids
told him. In fact, she'd never shown up at all. It wasn't
like her, he said. Coach was very mad.

Brian broke into a cold sweat, and ran to Numbles's house.

But of course Numbles wasn't there, and Jeremy,

shooting baskets in the driveway, hadn't seen Darcy either.

"Okay if I wait for your brother?" Brian asked Jeremy.

"Sure." Jeremy tossed him the ball. "How about a little one-on-one?"

An hour later, when Numbles finally got home from his field trip, Brian followed him into his collecting room, where Numbles deposited a large frog in one of his tanks. "Oh, brother," he said when Brian told him what he'd seen in the house, and about Darcy. "She probably decided to do the job herself. All action and no thought—what did I tell you? We'll probably find her digging up the graves since you said she wasn't at the house."

But they didn't.

There was still no sign of her at the deserted house when they went back there, at least not in the yard. Steeling himself, Brian pushed the door open again, and led Numbles inside. Numbles walked gingerly, as if on a bed of nails, and averted his eyes when Brian went into the living room and checked out the crates again.

Everything was just as it had been a few hours earlier.

"At least they can't hurt her in the daytime," Brian whispered.

"But they can hurt us," Numbles whispered back, pulling Brian into the empty kitchen. "Or her if she comes nosing around here. I just remembered what it is if they see you looking at them when they're in their coffins or boxes or whatever. It's not that you'll become a vampire right away. It's that they'll hunt you down—stalk you—till they find you. Then they'll attack and you'll become a vampire if you die."

Brian shuddered involuntarily.

"They didn't look at me," Numbles went on. "But you said that kid one looked as if he was looking at you. The woman, too, maybe; I think it's hard to tell if they see you or not when they're—well, sort of sleeping. And"—Numbles's voice broke—"I bet they looked at Tex. I bet that's what the big male one is doing now—finishing him off." He turned away, then whirled back again, facing Brian. "Hey, wait a minute! How can a vampire be out in daylight?"

"He must be in Grandpop's barn, in that dirt pile, remember? The note said 'In barn today.' Come on, let's have a look around the other rooms."

Numbles caught hold of Brian's arm. "One way or another," he said, "we've got to get rid of them. It's not just your grandmother and the cows. You—you're a marked man now, Brian."

Brian cleared his throat. "Yes," he said. "I know."

Huddled close together, the two boys crept through the rest of the house—dining room, pantry, bathrooms, second- and third-floor bedrooms, even the cellar.

But there was no sign of either Darcy or Tex.

THE PLAN

AFTER DINNER AT the farm, while his grandparents were watching TV, Brian went upstairs to pack for his overnight visit to Numbles's house. But first he quietly took his garlic bottles into Grandmom's room and smeared the juice around the door frame and the window frame. He wanted to put some on the bedposts, too, but he was afraid Grandmom would smell it that close up and either wash it off or move out of her room. As a precaution, he also did the guest room, which Grandpop was still using as a bedroom.

By then, both bottles were empty. He wondered about getting some more for himself, and for Numbles and Darcy, but he decided to wait till they'd worked out their plan. It wouldn't do for the vampires to smell garlic on them ahead of time and get suspicious.

He threw the empty bottles away in his own room, under some used tissues, washed his hands thoroughly, and packed.

"Okay, Grandpop," he called cheerfully, taking his suitcase downstairs. "I'm all set to go."

By nine o'clock that night, after another thunderstorm, there was still no sign of Darcy, and her parents, who had already phoned all the neighbors, called the police. The coach had gotten up a search party, Jeremy was pasting old photos of her on posterboard—and Brian and Numbles sat disconsolately in Numbles's room, alternately looking out in the direction of the empty house and trying to devise a plan—a rescue plan now, as well as a vampire-catching one.

"Maybe Cadge could help," Numbles suggested. "Maybe if we took him an old pair of her socks or something."

Brian shook his head. "I'm pretty sure Cadge is scared to death of the vampires. If they've got Darcy, he won't be any help at all."

"Yeah, of course." Numbles got up and leaned out the window for the hundredth time; they had raised the screen so they could see out farther. "I remember now. Domestic animals are supposed to be afraid of the supernatural."

Brian nodded, remembering all the times Cadge had shied away from the dead cows. If only he'd known that earlier . . .

"Hey," said Numbles suddenly. "What was that?" He leaned farther out the window.

Brian stood up; he'd heard it, too—a muffled scream, it sounded like, coming from down the street.

He heard it again.

"Darcy!" he shouted. "Let's go!" Without waiting for Numbles to extract himself from the window, he ran out of the room, down the stairs, and outdoors.

Numbles caught up with him in the driveway, where they heard the scream again, and then, as they approached the empty house, they heard sounds of frantic scuffling coming from the back yard. As they rounded the corner by the steps, Brian could just make out—it was quite dark now—two people struggling there: a large figure, draped in what looked like a cloak, and a smaller one whose bare limbs flashed in what little light there was.

"Darcy!" shouted Numbles. "We're coming! Hang on!"

"We've got the stakes!" Brian yelled, thinking quickly. "Sharp and ready. Hold onto him for us, will you?"

There was a muffled but horrible roar that curdled Brian's blood. And then, with a final wrenching twist, the smaller figure separated itself from the larger one, and the larger one—vanished.

"Where'n heck did he go?" asked Darcy, blinking, brushing off her hands. "Hey, did you see that karate move? I chopped him a good one, right in the . . ."

"Where *did* he go?" said Brian, confused.

Numbles pointed to a thin smoke-like substance rising from the house's outside wall, collecting itself and slipping under the back door. "Mist," he said. "Remember?"

"Oh, good grief," said Brian. "Of course."

"Well, he sure wasn't mist when we were fighting," said Darcy. "And it was my karate chop that freed me."

"No doubt," Numbles remarked dryly. "And I suppose that wasn't you screaming before?"

"Screaming? I may have *shouted* to alert passersby, but . . ."

Numbles snorted.

"So," said Darcy, "where are the stakes?"

"That was a ruse," Brian told her. "To scare him away. I'm surprised it worked, since it's hours till daylight and he wasn't in his grave or anything."

"Family," said Numbles. "Probably worried we'd gotten the wife and kid before the sun went down."

"Sheesh." Darcy looked disappointed. "Here we are, great opportunity and all, and you guys forget your stakes. Mine's around here somewhere." She stuck her tongue out at Numbles. "I made myself a new one."

"Darcy." Brian led her around the hedge and into her own yard; Numbles followed. "As I was just pointing out, stakes probably won't work if the vampire's not in his grave or his coffin or something. Which he sure wasn't. Just what were you going to do, anyway?"

Darcy's mouth twitched. "I was just staking out the house."

"Very funny," said Numbles. "*Staking* out. Almost as good as *pointing* out. When you two finish punning, maybe we can . . . Ohmigosh!" He broke off, staring at Darcy. "Is that blood on your neck?"

Darcy reached up a hand, and Brian stared, too, now; her finger came away bloodstained and Brian saw a small oozing wound on one side of her neck.

"He can't have gotten much," Brian said shakily, reaching out a hand to Darcy. "And it's okay, you know; he didn't kill you. You can't become a vampire after just one little bite. Not unless you die of it."

"Right," said Darcy. But she looked at her finger as if mesmerized. "I told you they were after me," she whispered. "And it seemed like you were taking forever to do anything about it. So I—well, I thought I'd hang around the house and just see if any of them came out. I thought if I was quick enough with my stake I might be able to surprise one. But that big one surprised me. He was on his way in instead of out."

"Didn't you see us looking for you?" Numbles asked angrily. "The whole town's been looking for you!"

"I know. I'm sorry. I went into the woods to make my stake because I didn't want to be seen, and I was here in the bushes later when you guys came by. But I couldn't blow my cover. Hey, what did you see inside?"

They told her.

"Wow," she said enviously. "Sheesh, I wish I *had* blown my cover and gone in with you."

"Teach you a lesson," said Numbles under his breath.

Darcy gave him a dirty look. "But it's just as well I was out here," she said, "because I had plenty of time to think, and I got this really neat idea."

"Oh, terrific," said Numbles sarcastically. "Let me guess. First we get some baseball bats . . ."

Brian kicked him. "We could use some new ideas. What was it, Darce?"

"Well, I suddenly thought maybe we wouldn't have to stake them after all. I mean I brought my new stake and everything, but the more I thought of doing it, the more I thought about how yucky it'd be and what if we missed and all, and then" — she turned to Numbles — "Numb, isn't it true that if you keep a vampire out after sunrise he just sort of, well, disappears?"

"Yeah," said Numbles dubiously. "It's supposed to be true. But staking's safer, I think. More reliable."

"So what?" said Darcy. "It's also harder. It seems to me the other's worth a try, at least. At first when he attacked me, I thought maybe I could hold him off till dawn . . ."

"Darcy, you're very brave," Brian interrupted. "But it's only around ten now. Dawn's hours and hours away. And George Knowles is a pretty big guy."

"I know." Darcy rubbed her shoulder.

Numbles was looking nervously at the house and at the kitchen door, which Brian now saw was slightly ajar. "Let's get out of here," Numbles said. "It's not the best place to talk about plans. What if they hear us?"

"Yeah," said Darcy. "I need a Coke anyway. And I guess I'd better go in and say hi to my folks. Why don't I do that and then we can meet back at your place, Numbles? Your folks are going to start wondering about you, too, pretty soon."

"Will your mom let you out again?" asked Brian, knowing his never would. But maybe people who sent their kids to boarding school acted differently.

"If she doesn't, I'll get out anyway. Just give me about twenty minutes for the lecture, that's all. Okay? See ya." With a jaunty wave, Darcy sprinted around the side of her house and up the porch steps.

"There's the grain trick," said Numbles slowly as he and Brian walked back to his house.

"Huh?"

"You scatter oats or something like that on their doorstep and for some reason they have to count each grain. Do it close enough to dawn when they're coming home and they're still counting when the sun comes up. Then, poof, no more vampire, supposedly. But where do we get oats?"

"It's not so much that," said Brian. "I'm sure Grandpop or one of the other farmers has some. But with all the thunderstorms we've been having, wouldn't the grains stick together if they got wet and turn into mush? Then the vampires probably wouldn't have to count them. The grains also might just plain wash away."

"Yeah," said Numbles moodily. "Yeah, you're probably right. The grain might stay dry if we put it on the front porch, but since the vampires seem to use the back door, there'd be no point in that. And since there's no roof over the back steps, the grain *would* get wet if it rained. So that's no good. Blast it! It's too much of a risk."

Half an hour later, the three of them were sitting around the table in Numbles's collecting room, and twenty minutes after that they had thought of and discarded at least five different plans, including the oats one.

"I still think we should try my idea," Darcy insisted. "Keeping them out till sunrise, I mean."

"Oh, come on, Darcy," said Numbles disgustedly. "How're we going to do that? We can't very well engage them in pleasant conversation—they'd attack. They've seen both you and Brian, remember, at least the kid one saw Brian, and the man saw you—maybe all of us. Besides, if we tried force they'd fight back, and even with your karate, we're not strong enough to overpower them. Vampires have superhuman strength."

"Yeah," said Darcy, rubbing her shoulder again and then fingering a small white bandage on her neck. "I guess you're right." She sighed and then went past Brian to one of the cages and peered inside.

Numbles joined her. "He's new," he said. "A Southwestern earless lizard, *Holbrookia texana scitula*, kind of like that lizard they called an iguana in the movie the other night, remember? My uncle sent him to me; I just got him yesterday. Isn't he a beauty?"

"Sure, Numbles," said Darcy. "A real knockout. He looks as if he's dressed up for . . ." Her eyes widened and she shouted, "That's it! I've got it. Oh, boy, oh, boy, oh, boy, do I ever have it! Listen, we won't be able to do it till tomorrow night, because we'll have to invite them first, but I think I've got the perfect plan."

Numbles raised his eyebrows at Brian. "Yeah?" he said. "So what is it?"

Darcy sat down, clearly savoring being the center of attention. "Well," she began, "we want to keep the vampires out till sunrise, right?"

"Right," said Brian impatiently. "I thought we'd more or less come up with that already. But we can't do it by force, Darcy; we've been through that."

Darcy ignored him. "So what better way to keep people out late than a party?"

Brian and Numbles exchanged another look. "Sure, Darce," Numbles said indulgently. "Sure. All we have to do," he said to Brian, as if explaining the obvious, "is invite them over, serve Cokes and chips and stuff, put on some really great music, and . . ."

"Never mind the Cokes and chips," said Brian. "We'll be the refreshments."

"Not if we're vampires, too," said Darcy.

The boys stared at her.

"We could dress up," she said. "We could make black capes, and use theatrical makeup to disguise who we are and to make our faces real pale. My mom has some," she explained to Brian. "She's in community theater. And we could make vampire teeth . . ."

"Oh, brother," said Numbles. "First of all, it's a dumb idea. Second . . ."

"Hang on a sec," Brian interrupted. "I hate parties, too, but—what would you make teeth out of, Darce?"

Darcy shrugged. "Chalk. Squash. I think I've even got a set of plastic ones, left over from a couple of Halloweens ago. Maybe some other kids around do, too. We'll manage. Well?" she said triumphantly. "What do you think?"

"We'd be taking an awful risk," said Brian slowly.

"We could wear garlic bulbs under our clothes," said Numbles equally slowly.

"What if they slip out?" asked Darcy. "Or smell?"

Brian sighed. "You're right. No garlic. So we're back to its being a big risk."

"Plus dumb," said Numbles. He held up his hand as Brian started to protest. "I know, I know. We haven't thought of anything better."

"The thing is," Brian told him, "in the dark we might just be able to get away with it. The disguises, I mean. Especially if Darcy's mom has all that makeup."

"What if there's a full moon?" said Numbles. He consulted a calendar. "Okay. There won't be. But . . ."

"Numbles," said Brian quietly. "It's either that or staking them. We're desperate."

"Yeah." He slapped the calendar down. "Yeah, we are."

"All *right!*" Darcy shouted. She pulled her chair closer to the table. "Now we've got to work out the details."

"What," said Brian, "do you suppose vampires do at parties?"

Numbles gave a short unenthusiastic laugh. "That's easy," he said. "Play spin the tombstone, pin the tail on the werewolf—stuff like that."

"How will we invite them?"

Both boys turned to Darcy.

"A note, I guess." Then she grinned. "Written in blood, like the note you saw, Brian. We could say we were long-lost cousins or something."

"No," said Brian. "They must know who their relatives are."

"Well—well . . ."

"We could say," Numbles put in, "that we'd heard about their near-triumph over the Larrabee family and wanted to congratulate them. Give them a little celebration."

"That might work." Brian turned it over in his mind, examining it from all sides, Holmes-like. "Yeah. It might work."

"Yippee!" cried Darcy. "Now was that a good idea or was that a good idea?"

"Yeah, yeah," Numbles said. "It was a good idea. Hey—we better make a list. I think my mom's got some old black cloth . . ."

Brian went back to the farm first thing the next morning, and was relieved to see that Grandmom was no worse, although she said there had been a funny smell in the room and flapping noises outside her window. The dreams were much better, though, she said. Brian went upstairs and sniffed at her window frame while she was in the living room. There was still some garlic smell, but it had faded a lot; he'd have to get some more juice for that night. Then he hurried outside, did his chores, and went back to the village to meet Numbles and Darcy.

The teeth were the hardest part, they discovered, once they started their preparations. Capes were easy. Even Brian was able to sew a sort of a hem in the top of his, and poke a bright red drawstring through it, made from some decorative braid Darcy's mom had. Numbles, whose father had once been in an old-fashioned wedding, found a black top hat. They all had sneakers, which they covered with black shoe polish, and Darcy's mother's makeup box had plenty of Clown White and Pale Juvenile, which mixed together made a wonderfully sickly color. She also had some iridescent goo that glowed green in the dark, but they were pretty sure that vampires didn't glow—the Knowleses didn't seem to, anyway—and as Numbles said, "It wouldn't do to have to explain why we're different from your average everyday garden-variety vampire."

But the teeth—that was a stumper. Chalk was easy to whittle to a point, but hard to fasten and too bulky, not to mention unpleasant-tasting. Pale summer squash was better, for you could cut a tooth-shape easily, but it was hard to fasten, too, and the wrong color besides. Darcy's plastic teeth were fine for her, but no one else she or Numbles knew had any, and the local drugstore, which was the main supplier of party goods, didn't have its Halloween items in yet.

"Cardboard?" suggested Brian uncertainly; they were sitting gloomily around Numbles's kitchen table that afternoon, discussing the problem. "Clay?"

"What are you guys up to?" asked Jeremy, coming into the room and reaching up to the cupboard. "Want some peanut butter?"

Darcy looked hopeful for a moment but then shook her head. "It wouldn't hold its shape," she said. "And neither would clay or cardboard once they got wet enough. Besides, peanut butter's the wrong color."

Jeremy gave her a strange look and then plunked a large jar down on the table along with some strawberry jam and a loaf of bread. Brian immediately picked up a slice and tore it into quarters, then molded each quarter into a tooth shape.

"Holds more peanut butter whole," said Jeremy, spreading a generous knifeful onto an intact slice, adding jam, and taking a huge bite.

"We weren't thinking of eating it, numbskull," said Numbles scornfully. "We were . . ."

". . . working out Halloween costumes in advance," said Darcy, kicking Brian under the table; he got the idea and kicked Numbles, who was next to him.

"Huh?" said Numbles. "Hey, that hurt!"

"What did?" asked Jeremy.

Brian rolled his eyes significantly toward Jeremy and at last Numbles's face brightened. "Oh, yeah, Halloween!" he exclaimed. "Right. Costumes, Jeremy, costumes."

Jeremy stared at him. "A peanut butter mask?" he asked incredulously.

"Not quite," said Numbles. "You see . . ."

"Of course," said Darcy, swinging her leg farther this time; Brian saw Numbles recoil from the blow. "With bits of bread stuck on it for eyes. Hey, shouldn't you be working out, Jer? Shooting some baskets, maybe? How about that record you were trying to break? Gotta keep training, you know."

"What record?" Jeremy finished his sandwich and screwed the cap back on the peanut butter jar. "Oh, you mean Marty White's thirty-seven baskets in a row. I beat it already. Yesterday."

"Hey, all right!" Darcy thumped him on the back. "Way to go, Jeremy!"

Numbles groaned, and rubbed his leg. "How about you see if you can beat your own record, then?"

he said to his brother. "Go for thirty-eight. Go for fifty."

Jeremy put the two jars away and threw his gooey knife into the sink. "Nope," he said. "I gotta go brush my teeth. I had two cavities at the dentist's today. See ya!"

"Mmm," said Darcy, and Brian waved.

"I know!" said Numbles, snapping his fingers. "Plaster. Or spackling compound."

"Isn't that stuff poisonous?" asked Brian.

Numbles's face fell. "Yeah, you're right. I think plaster is, anyway."

"*I* know!" Darcy had been looking thoughtfully after Jeremy, and now she pushed her chair back with a tremendous clatter. "I've got it! Come on!"

She led the mystified boys outside and down a side street, where a neat yellow house surrounded by a picket fence sat in the middle of a wide expanse of lawn. A small sign above a side entrance read: DR. CATCHWAY, D.M.D.

"Oh, come on, Darcy," said Numbles. "You're old enough to go to the dentist by yourself."

"I'm not going to the dentist, you are," she said, pushing him and Brian inside and into a small waiting room. "See, Numb, Jeremy's some use after all." She held her wristwatch up so it faced them. "It's three o'clock; that's just about when Catchway stops having appointments in the summer. Cheer up, Numbles; you know you like him. He'll understand."

"Yeah, but I'm not sure I do," said Numbles under his breath as a starched hygienist came out of an inner office and smiled at them. "Why, Darcy Dixie!" she exclaimed. "Edward! We just saw your brother Jeremy this morning, Edward. How nice to see you, too. Not a toothache, I hope?" She looked anxiously at both of them and then at Brian.

"No, Miss Fleckle, no," said Darcy sweetly. "We're all fine. But we do have a professional question to ask Dr. Catchway."

"He'll be through in a minute," said Miss Fleckle. "Have a seat."

"Darcy, what are you up to?" Brian whispered, sitting gingerly on the edge of a straight-backed chair. "I *hate* dentists, I really do."

"This won't hurt," said Darcy. "At least I don't think it will." She looked smug. "Where else would you go for false teeth," she said, "but to a dentist? I'm just glad Jeremy was around to give me the idea."

Numbles stood up. "Oh, no, you don't," he said, starting for the door. "Not in my mouth. They pull teeth before they give you false ones, you jerk. Come on, Brian!"

Darcy pushed him back into his chair. "I don't mean real false teeth," she snarled. "I mean fake ones. Ones you can wear over your regular teeth, or around them, or something. Dr. Catchway'll know how. Come on, Numbles, you know he's a good guy."

He did seem okay, Brian thought when Dr. Catchway stepped out into the waiting room, ushering out a fussy-looking elderly lady. He was tall and slender; young, with bright blue eyes that looked perpetually amused, and a great shock of shaggy hair.

"Darcy!" he exclaimed when the old lady had left. "Numbles! How the heck are you?" He shook hands with each of them.

"This is Brian," said Darcy, pushing him forward. "He's visiting. From New York."

"New York, eh?" said Dr. Catchway. "Still as noisy as ever? I went to dental school there, but I moved back here when I realized I preferred moos to sirens. So—what can I do for you folks?"

"Well," said Darcy, "we're going to this dress-up party tonight, and we thought it would be really neat to go as vampires. All of us. We have capes and stuff— we've spent just about all day on them—and my mom has this great theatrical makeup, and I have some plastic teeth, but the guys don't. We tried squash and chalk, but they didn't work, and we've ruled out plaster and clay and cardboard."

Dr. Catchway's sparkling eyes sparkled even more. "And of course what's a vampire without long teeth?" he said. "I see. Let me think. How long do these teeth have to last?"

"Several hours," said Numbles.

"A really lot of hours," said Darcy.

"All night," said Brian, figuring if they said anything less, the teeth might fall apart and expose them prematurely.

Dr. Catchway gave Darcy a narrow look. "I see. Of course," he asked casually, "your folks know about this party?"

"Oh, yes," lied Darcy without flinching. What an actress, Brian thought; maybe she comes by it naturally, with her mom in community theater.

"I think I have just the thing," said Dr. Catchway, his sparkle returning. "That is, if you fellahs don't mind a few minutes in the dentist's chair."

Brian hated every second of it, though it didn't hurt. The goo Dr. Catchway put into his mouth tasted vile, like fake peppermint, and he had to sit very still. But a couple of hours later when they went back, he and Numbles each had a convincing set of vampire teeth that fit snugly over their own canines — strong, firm, sharp, and great-looking.

"Hey, this is sort of like the retainer I used to have to wear," said Numbles, sliding his set out and examining the acrylic band that held them together.

"Right," said Dr. Catchway. "That's just what it is — a vampire retainer."

"Um — what do we owe you?" Brian asked, his voice a bit muffled by his teeth.

"A full report on how the teeth hold up," said Dr. Catchway, showing them to the door. "Who knows? I might decide to go into the vampire-tooth business on the side. We'll call this a test run. No apples," he called after them. "No steak, either. Have fun!"

THE ATTACK

FUN ISN'T EXACTLY what I'd call it, Brian thought hours later, shifting uncomfortably in his long cape. Still, Holmes was known for his disguises; Brian only hoped his would be as convincing as his idol's.

Brian had met Numbles and Darcy about an hour before sunset, after all three of them had given various not entirely truthful alibis to their families, and after Brian had given Grandmom's room another garlic treatment. They had sneaked inside the empty house cautiously and Brian had tacked their invitation to the largest crate while Numbles and Darcy huddled in the kitchen. All three vampires were "at home," and looked more awake than they had the last time he'd seen them; Brian covered his face and his hand shook annoyingly as he delivered the invitation, which had cost all three of them several pricked fingers to write.

It said:

CONGRATULATIONS ON YOUR CAMPAIGN AGAINST THE
LARRABEES, WHICH WE UNDERSTAND IS NEARING
COMPLETION. WE ARE FRIENDS WHO HAVE SIMILAR
TASTES AND WOULD LIKE TO CELEBRATE YOUR SUC-
CESS WITH YOU TONIGHT. AS WE ARE YOUNGER THAN
YOU (MOST OF YOU) WE WOULD APPRECIATE ANY TIPS
YOU CAN GIVE US.
THREE HOURS AFTER MIDNIGHT. AT YOUR GRAVES.
SINCERELY,
THREE FRIENDS

They'd decided to meet the vampires so late because that would give them less time to fill before
dawn. Darcy had wanted to sign the invitation
"FRIENDS IN BLOOD," but Brian and Numbles had
vetoed that on the grounds that vampires might not
talk that way among themselves.

Now, dressed in their unfamiliar clothes and trying
to stay awake and master the art of talking around
their new teeth, they were waiting in the dim light of
a half-moon for their guests, after a tense walk through
the graveyard, past the Angel of Death statue, to the
Knowleses' graves.

"It's quarter past three," Darcy whispered around
her teeth, yawning and pulling her cape tighter. The
weather had turned suddenly cool—although that was
normal for Vermont in late August, Brian remembered from his previous visits.

"Shh, what's that?" asked Brian, instantly wide

awake. Surely that was a footstep—another—and another . . .

"Good evening," a sonorous voice intoned, and a
tall, gaunt caped figure in a top hat emerged from
behind a curve in the path, followed by a shorter, more
rounded one and a much smaller one.

The tall figure bowed and swept off his hat. Numbles did the same. "Mr. Knowles, I presume?" he said,
holding out a gloved hand—they had decided gloves
would be a better disguise than Mrs. Verona's body
makeup. Besides, body makeup might come off and
give them away. "What a pleasure!"

"A great pleasure," said Darcy, making a clumsy
curtsy and smiling; her red lips looked black in the
dim light. "Mrs. Knowles, may I congratulate you
personally? And this must be your son."

The kid vampire, who looked to be about seven or
eight, held something tightly against his chest. "Hi,"
he said sullenly. "Meet Son of Dracula." He thrust
out what he'd been holding.

It was Tex.

Brian quickly moved closer to Numbles, who had
made a choking sound. "Very interesting," he said
politely. "What is it?"

Mr. Knowles shrugged. "Some kind of reptile," he
said. "Georgie—my son—was doing some prelimi-
nary research on a possible—er—client, and he ran
into it. Found it irresistible, in fact. It is of great interest to us because it emits blood from its eyes when
disturbed. Show them, Georgie."

Brian kept a firm grip on Numbles's arm while Georgie poked Tex with a stick, holding him tightly with the other hand, because of course poor Tex struggled. Suddenly two red jets shot from Tex's eyes, spattering Numbles.

Darcy rushed forward, grabbed Numbles by the shoulders, and pretended to slurp the blood off his cape.

"My apologies," she said, as if embarrassed. "I have not dined."

Mrs. Knowles's eyes gleamed. "Good," she said in a grating voice. "It is good that you did that." She folded her cape around her and sat down on her own tombstone—but her eyes remained alert, darting from one of them to the other. "You see, we have had—some trouble lately, and we were not sure when we got your invitation . . ."

"Daddy had a sort of a fight with some small person," said Georgie. "And this kid come into our house, the kid from the farm, I mean, a couple of times. I couldn't see the face of the one who brought the invitation, though. I guess it was you, huh? But I thought it might be him again. You're the same size."

"Of course," said Mr. Knowles, watching the three of them closely, "if it had been a trick, we could easily have prevailed. It's a rare mortal who can withstand a vampire attack at night."

Brian heard Darcy snicker faintly, but she stopped when Mr. Knowles's lips curled back and he fingered one of his long teeth as if in warning.

"How true," said Mrs. Knowles, rubbing her hands together. Her nails, Brian saw, were painted a dark color and filed into cruel-looking V-shaped points.

"If it'd been that kid," said Georgie, "I'd have finished him off real quick." He grinned nastily. His canine teeth were small, but looked needle-sharp, like a kitten's.

"Georgie is a light sleeper," said his mother. "We rely on him to keep watch for us." She patted a spot next to her on the tombstone, just about where the date was; her nails clicked on the hard surface. "Come," she said to Darcy, crooning the words, "do sit down. Make yourself—comfortable."

Darcy didn't move. Mrs. Knowles glared at her for a moment, and then, after a glance at her husband, asked suspiciously, "How long have you been undead, child?"

"Oh," said Darcy, gulping and edging closer to the boys, "a couple of ye . . ."

Brian stepped heavily on her foot.

". . . of weeks," she corrected herself. "But I don't think I've really gotten the knack of it yet."

"And who enlisted you?" asked Mr. Knowles, towering above her and looking down menacingly; she's got to get away from him, thought Brian.

"Well, I . . ." Darcy sputtered. "You see, I . . ." She clutched at her mouth then and turned a horrified face to Brian.

Oh, no—her teeth! thought Brian, stepping quickly

in front of her. If they go, he'll know we're faking—
maybe he'll even recognize her. He poked Numbles,
who was still staring at Tex, and at the same time
said, stalling, "We're not sure, any of us, actually,
who—um—enlisted us. Not exactly, anyway." He
poked Numbles again.

"You know how it is," said Numbles finally. "Vague
dreams. Fog. Mist . . ."

"Yes, mist," said Brian, wishing that Darcy, who
was still behind him, would stop poking frantically at
her mouth and apply her total concentration to helping convince the vampires that the three of them were
vampires, too. "You try to sleep, and you're not sure
if you're asleep or not . . ."

"Right," said Numbles dreamily. "How true. And
you—you're sort of weak, and you think you see . . ."

"Bats," said Brian. "I remember one bat," he went
on, desperately glancing around at Darcy, who with
one hand gestured him to turn back while she fished
in her mouth with the other. ". . . one bat, huge, he
was, and very black, and his eyes were very bright,
and I—I . . ."

"You sank back," said Darcy at last, flashing a toothy
grin at Brian as she sprang forward, "didn't you, and
then you began to see a person, you know, forming
out of the bat, gradually. I think mine was someone I
knew," she went on, closing her eyes dreamily, as if
relishing the memory, and waving one hand in an un-
characteristically ethereal gesture. "But he did come

as a bat, like—er—my friend's; I'm sure of that. He could have been one of my teachers, Mr. Sloan, maybe . . ." She snapped her eyes open dramatically and looked straight at Mrs. Knowles. "I like bat shape myself," she said matter-of-factly, "the flying especially, don't you? To be able to fly . . ."

"Hey," interrupted Georgie—not a moment too soon, Brian thought, till he heard what Georgie said: "Let's have a shapeshifting contest. I just learned mist, want to see?" Without waiting for an answer, he became transparent and began to vaporize. Tex fell to the ground, blinked, and then hopped unsteadily forward. Brian had to hold Numbles back to keep him from grabbing him.

"Georgie!" scolded Mrs. Knowles—but she looked a little less suspicious now. "Come back this instant!"

Georgie materialized again, and bent to pick up Tex, who had scurried under a corner of the tombstone and seemed to be suffering from a reptilian version of the shakes. "Bad Draccy-pooh," Georgie said, pouting. "I wish you'd learn to shapeshift with me."

"Perhaps," said Mr. Knowles—he was still watching them all closely, Brian noticed, especially Darcy—"a shapeshifting contest wouldn't be a bad idea."

"My husband does a wonderful wolf," said Mrs. Knowles. "Show them, dear."

Mr. Knowles nodded gravely, pulled his cloak over his face, and then drew in upon himself until he was short and elongated. Mist swirled around him, and Brian blinked—

—right into the eyes of a lean gray wolf, whose mouth was open, panting, slobbering, looming over him—

—And then the mist came again, and the wolf shape got taller and longer—

—until Mr. Knowles was back with them again, and Mrs. Knowles and Georgie were clapping.

"Th-that was very good," Brian managed. "Much better than anything we can do."

"You next," said Mrs. Knowles sweetly.

"Well—" said Brian.

"You see—" said Numbles.

"Boy, am I hungry!" said Darcy. "I could eat a horse."

"Perhaps," said Mr. Knowles dryly, with a glance at his wife, "we can find you one."

Darcy made a sound halfway between a cough and a gasp. "Thanks," she said, "but I—I'll go get one later. I—um—need the practice."

"Yes," said Brian quickly. "We want to hear about your campaign first, anyway. It sounds so, so . . ."

"So exciting," supplied Numbles. "And—instructive."

"And—and *delicious.*" Darcy smiled engagingly at Mrs. Knowles.

At that, Mrs. Knowles seemed to lose the last of her skepticism. "My dear, it is," she said with great enthusiasm. "Although cows are not really my cup of tea." Here she laughed, a shrill high-pitched cackle. "Revenge is sweet, though, as they say. It began . . ."

"Let me tell it, Christina," interrupted Mr. Knowles; he, too, seemed more inclined to accept them now, Brian thought. Or was it just that he was caught up in the prospect of telling his story? Don't trust him, Brian told himself; don't let your guard down . . .

"You see," Mr. Knowles began, "some time ago I was in Mr. Larrabee's employ. I did not know it then, but I had already been enlisted, at least partly, on a European trip. My recruiter was from Rumania and of the distinguished family of Vlad Tepes, known to the uninitiated as Dracula. He accompanied me here, ostensibly as a traveling companion, but actually to complete my enlistment and to seek new blood. As he drew me closer into the fold, I found it difficult to keep any regular employment, for of course, as we all understand, I was growing increasingly listless during the day."

Mrs. Knowles cackled again, and put an arm around her son, who seemed to be fascinated by Darcy's teeth; had they slipped again? Brian couldn't see.

"As time went on, I could perform my tasks less and less, but Mr. Larrabee did not sympathize. Looking back, I suppose I see his point, for I neglected to close gates and to bring the cows in for milking more than once; I was sleepy and weak. He suggested I see a doctor, and when I would not—for by now I was aware of what was happening—he took the entire matter as a disciplinary one. 'George,' he used to say, 'you seem like an educated man. If you will not seek medical aid, I have no recourse but to fire you.' I pleaded with him, for I badly needed the money to support my family, but he would have none of it.

"I was dismissed, and in due course I ceased to live, and immediately began enlisting my wife and son. They soon followed, and you know the rest."

"Not quite," said Brian quickly. "Why the cows? Why not just the Larrabees themselves?"

Mr. Knowles's lips curled into a sneer. "As I was slowly made to suffer humiliation by being admonished for not doing my work, I wished Larrabee also to suffer slowly. The cows are his livelihood, and I was poor when I no longer worked for him. I wanted him to feel the pain of poverty also, and the pinch of terror. I wanted him to worry about his family as I had worried about mine. The battle was joined even more one evening recently when I was in his barn, in bat shape, and again even more recently when an odor that is deeply repugnant to us all was affixed to some of his bedroom doors and windows." He chuckled chillingly. "But we will let them think they have foiled us, and then simply enter another way."

Georgie turned to Brian. "The kid wasn't there when the smell was," he said. "The Larrabee kid. He's the one who came to the house. There wasn't any smell in his room, though, so I could've gotten him if he'd been there. I would've, too!"

"Another time," said Mrs. Knowles soothingly. "Live children spend the night with their friends now and then, don't you remember?"

"He would have been my first," said Georgie petulantly. "I'm sick of drinking out of a cup, like a baby. I want to use these." He bared his teeth again, and Brian dug his knee into Darcy's back as she recoiled, her face twisting.

For once, Mr. Knowles seemed not to have noticed. He took a bottle out from under his cape, and said, "I have brought some of the best vintage. A taste for each of us, to celebrate." His eyes glittered as he held the bottle up, displaying it to them. It's a test, Brian said to himself; I was right not to trust him.

"Spit it out," whispered Numbles, while Mr. Knowles was busy with the cork. "Don't swallow it. I think it'll taint you."

Brian, trying to ignore the nausea that welled up inside him, took the bottle from Mr. Knowles, put his mouth to it, and tipped it up. I could just pretend, he thought, and not even put any in my mouth—but the bottle's full; they'd know. Well, maybe if I take some, the others can just pretend.

Closing his eyes and holding his breath, he poured a little of the thick salty liquid into his mouth and tried not to think of where—or who—it might have come from. Then he passed the bottle to Darcy. As she turned to one side, tipping her head back, Brian pretended to cover a cough with his cape, and spat the blood out into it. "Delicious!" he said, and then panicked; suppose it was a trick and it wasn't blood at all?

But the vampires seemed satisfied, and Darcy passed the bottle to Numbles.

Brian sneaked a look at his watch when Numbles had returned the bottle and there was an awkward pause. It was only a little after four o'clock. How were they going to keep the vampires busy till sunrise?

While the Knowleses were drinking from the bottle themselves, Brian pulled at Darcy's cape and gestured toward his watch.

Darcy looked at him blankly for a moment, but then comprehension showed in her eyes and she said to the vampires, "There must be so much you could teach us. You—you said your recruiter was from Dracula's family . . ."

"The family of Vlad Tepes," Mr. Knowles corrected coldly. "If you are to be one of us, you must use the name we use—the correct name."

"Sorry," Darcy said humbly. "But could you tell us more about him? About Vlad—Vlad Tepes?"

"I thought," Mr. Knowles said, eyeing her narrowly, "that you were hungry."

"Well, yes," said Darcy, pivoting quickly to face Brian and Numbles, and mouthing *Help!* in the second during which she faced them. "I am, that is I was, but . . ."

"The—er—drink you gave us was so good," said Brian hastily. "We can wait."

"Well, I cannot," said Mr. Knowles shortly. "Will you excuse me?"

"Sure," said Brian, thinking, we should have offered refreshments. But relieved, too; the thought of what he might have had to eat made his stomach feel like a closing fist.

"Perhaps," said Mrs. Knowles, sounding almost friendly, "when my husband returns he will tell us some of the old tales he learned in Rumania."

"Hey, that'd be great!" said Darcy, and Brian sneaked another look at his watch. Not much progress. He hoped Mr. Knowles knew a lot of very interesting stories.

There was a brief scuffle in one corner of the graveyard and a muffled yowl. A moment later, Mr. Knowles came back carrying a couple of small limp bodies. "Ordinarily I do not bother with cats," he explained. "The blood is thin, and there is not much of it. But they are so plentiful, handy when one is in a hurry or just wants a simple snack. These struggled a bit too much, so I had to finish them off prematurely, but at least they are fresh." He turned to his family, putting a furry body in Mrs. Knowles's lap and a smaller one in his son's. Mrs. Knowles seized hers greedily and bent her head to its neck; Brian had to look away.

"There are several more," Mr. Knowles said to Brian. "I would have brought you some, but you said the drink satisfied you for now. Still—it is a long time till tomorrow's sunset, and as you said yourself, you must practice." He gave Darcy an oily smile.

"Yes." Brian stood up. "Yes, we must. So perhaps now you will excuse us for a moment." He pulled Numbles, who was pale even under his pale makeup, to his feet, then shook his head slightly at Darcy as she began to get up, too.

"After you," she said in a second, nodding imperceptibly, but looking more than a little uncomfortable. "You guys go ahead. I'm still pretty full."

Brian hurried Numbles through the underbrush. "I figured one of us had better stay," he explained, "so they can't slip off. Shoo!" He pushed a cat aside. "Get out of here, for Pete's sake! The thing is," he said, turning back to Numbles, "we need another plan. They're going to try to get away at dawn if we don't make the party so lively they forget. So far, it isn't much of a party. Come on—how do we keep them here?"

"I don't know."

"Well, I don't either."

"Why don't you ask Darcy?" suggested Numbles. "She's the one who thought of this."

"Darcy's not here."

"Yeah, I noticed." Numbles poked at some sticks with his toe. "I can't think of anything. We've just got to keep them busy, I guess."

"We could walk them home," Brian said slowly, "if they try to leave early. Then we could try to stall them at the door. Run ahead and block it, even, if we have to."

"They'll turn to mist and go under it."

"You're right. Darn! We should've stuffed something under it. Or put garlic juice on it."

"I'll go back now," said Numbles, "and stuff it. Tell them I was really starving and went off after more than a cat. Brian? Try to get Tex? Please?"

Brian promised, then called after him, "Both doors. Windows, too. All you can reach. And hurry!"

Then he went back to the others.

". . . so there he was," Mr. Knowles was saying, "this handsome young man, ready to go on his world tour . . . Oh, there you are," he said to Brian. "I was just telling your friend the interesting story of 'The Vampyre,' by Polidori. It's a true story, you know. Where is your other friend?"

"He decided he was hungry for something big. Don't let me interrupt you."

"Very well," said Mr. Knowles. "This fine young man—but surely you want to go and eat now?" he said to Darcy.

"Oh—no. No. I do get very hungry, but I—I eat lightly. That—er—snack will hold me for a while, really. Besides, I don't want to miss any of your story!"

"As you wish," said Mr. Knowles. "Well, as I was saying . . ."

Brian kept one eye on the sky and the other on his watch as Mr. Knowles's voice droned on. Darcy gestured at him several times, as if asking where Numbles was, but Brian didn't see any way to communicate their plan without giving it away, so he just ignored her and hoped she'd catch on.

At last Mr. Knowles finished his story, yawned, and stood up, stretching. "Umm," he said, "unless I miss my guess, we'd better be going."

"I've been wondering," said Brian quickly—the sky was just beginning to lighten—"why you haven't been sleeping in your graves."

"Mommy, I'm tired," whined Georgie, stroking Tex, whom he'd been holding on his lap. "I wanna go home. Draccy-pooh's tired, too."

"Hush, dear, your father's talking."

"Simple," Mr. Knowles was saying. "With the cemetery such a public place, we were afraid people would notice us coming and going. As for you—you are residing in your graves?"

"Oh, no," said Darcy. "For the same reason. As a matter of fact, we weren't even buried here. When we became undead, we decided to come here where we aren't so well known. Fresh blood, you know," she said merrily—but her eyes, Brian could see, were anxious, and she mouthed *"Where's Numbles?"* at him behind her hand, faking a yawn.

"At the house," he mouthed back, yawning, too. *"It's okay."*

"That's just the false dawn, isn't it?" he said aloud. "I've noticed it around here; it looks like it's dawning, but it isn't. I was just wondering if you'd ever seen Dracula's castle, Vlad Tepes's castle, I mean."

"Oh, Daddy, yes," squeaked Georgie, perking up. "Yes, tell about the castle. The cobwebs and the rats and the wolves and the fancy coffins—it's neat! He's told me about it lots and lots and it's almost like I've been there!"

"Georgie," said Mr. Knowles. "Another time. We have to go; it's almost bedtime. Our friends must go, too."

But luckily by now Georgie had completely revived and wouldn't be stopped. He rattled on and on, still holding Tex on his lap, and prompted at intervals by Darcy and Brian, as the sky grew steadily lighter and his parents grew more and more visibly anxious and less and less polite. Finally, just as the first streak of pink showed above the horizon, Mr. Knowles picked his son unceremoniously up, tucked him under his arm, and set off rapidly across the cemetery toward the house.

Brian grabbed Darcy's hand and they followed. "Numbles is sealing the doors and the windows," he told her quickly, "so they can't turn to mist and escape inside that way."

Darcy looked at the sky. "We've got a few minutes still," she said nervously. "I wish we'd brought some grain or something after all. We didn't even have a thunderstorm."

"It's too late for grain."

"What about the chimney?" They were running now, a few feet behind the vampires, who were lumbering past the Angel of Death as if being undead somehow made them out of shape and as if there weren't time for them to shapeshift into faster creatures.

"I didn't think of that. No way to reach it, anyway. But I'm sure they'll try the door first; it'd be quicker. Come on! We've got to get there before they do, so we can bar that back door, and somehow keep them busy so they won't have time to turn into something else and go down the chimney."

"Okay." Darcy took off in her best base runner's sprint, pulling ahead of Brian immediately and then passing the vampires, waving and shouting something back at them.

The sky grew steadily pinker.

Ahead of him, Brian saw the vampires clamber over the stone wall. Mr. Knowles was still carrying his son and Georgie was still carrying Tex, while Mrs. Knowles panted and gasped close behind. Brian leaped over the wall seconds after she went over it, and he felt a thrill of relief when he saw Numbles and Darcy standing in front of the back door. He remained behind the vampires, though, to prevent their trying to go back to their graves.

"Excuse—us," panted Mr. Knowles to Numbles and Darcy. "But we all—must get under cover. You—have forgotten yourselves—you will have to shelter with us. You will not have your own soil, but we are all from the same land, so you may share ours. The door is unlocked. Kindly open it, please."

"No," said Brian, from his position behind the

vampires. He tore off his cape. "No, I think not."

Mr. Knowles wheeled and faced him, his complexion more ashen than before. "Wh—what?" he stammered. "You—you're . . ."

"Daddy, it's him!" shrieked Georgie. With a nasty hiss, he bared his teeth.

"Yes," said Brian clearly as the first rays of sun peeped above the horizon. "I am Brian Larrabee. And I am very much alive."

"Oh, please," said Mrs. Knowles, turning to Darcy with a sob. "Please." She took her son from her husband's arms. "Think of my boy, of the little one."

"That little one swiped my friend's pet horned lizard," said Darcy, grabbing Tex and thrusting him at Numbles. "And besides, he'll be better off dead than undead. You all will."

"Mist!" shouted Mr. Knowles. "Turn to mist!"

"It's no use," said Numbles, cradling Tex in his arms. "The house is sealed. There's no way you can get in. I even stopped up the keyholes."

"Then I will unstop them!" shouted Mr. Knowles. He pushed Numbles aside and rushed up the back steps, where Darcy was standing.

Darcy tore off her cloak and pulled down one side of her shirt collar, ripping the bandage off her wound. She stretched her neck toward Mr. Knowles. "Hungry?" she crooned. "Come on."

"No, Darcy!" Brian shouted, running to her. But Numbles grabbed him and pointed to the sky.

Just as Mr. Knowles reached for Darcy, the full light of the sun burst gloriously over the horizon, flooding the steps and the yard with light.

And the three vampires melted harmlessly away.

MONSTER HUNTERS

"THAT," said Brian later that morning, when they had finished a hearty breakfast at the Larrabees', "was one of the bravest things I've ever seen anyone do in my whole life." He slipped Cadge a piece of bacon. A whole one; after all, Cadge had provided him with one of the first clues. Once again he wished he'd recognized it sooner for what it was!

"Yeah." Numbles stroked Tex, who sat beside him under a portable heat lamp. "Yeah, Darcy, it really was. You're okay."

"You guys're pretty good yourselves," said Darcy modestly. "I'll hunt monsters with you any time."

"You know," said Brian thoughtfully, "that's not a bad idea. I know I didn't believe at first, and I know Holmes would scoff at it, but still, we saw what we saw. I wonder how many unsolved crimes there are that really were done by creatures like the Knowleses. Creatures no one believes in any more, so no one looks for them or even considers them. I mean if there really are vampires left in the world, what about other monsters—throwbacks, maybe, like you said, Numbles."

"You mean what I said about dragons maybe being dinosaurs? And that supposedly extinct fish? You don't have to convince me."

Darcy gently touched her wound. She'd left the bandage off and Brian could see that although it was healing well, it would probably leave a scar. "You don't have to convince me, either," she said. "Not any more." Then she stood up as Brian's grandmother came into the kitchen, still wearing the scarf, but loosely. "Hi, there, Mrs. Larrabee. How're you feeling?"

"Much better, thank you." Grandmom reached down and gave Cadge a pat, but kept her distance from Tex. "I had only a few dreams last night, and none of them were out of the ordinary. That blood transfusion the doctor gave me worked wonders. I guess I was just a little anemic after all. And"—she smiled—"I'm actually hungry this morning."

Brian leaped to the stove and turned the heat on under the frying pan. "Toss me those eggs, Numbles," he ordered. "Darcy, the bread's over there. Toaster's right next to it."

"I'll get the coffee," said Grandpop, coming in cheerfully and pouring a mugful for himself and another for his wife. He went to the window and looked out over his fields. "No dead cow this morning," he said softly. "That one in the barn is no worse, and the herd seems calmer than it's been in weeks. I wonder," he mused, turning back to them and sitting down, "if we're free of it at last. Whatever it was."

There were no more dead cows at all, and Grandmom grew steadily better. In a couple of days, she stopped wearing the scarf, though she, too, Brian could see, would have a scar on her neck. Soon Brian would have to go back to the city, to the swim team and the Holmes movies he realized he'd hardly missed at all. And Darcy would follow in another week to go to her fancy school down South. "Which leaves me and Tex," Numbles muttered on Brian's last afternoon, when the three of them had met in his collecting room for the last time. "And then Tex'll go, too, when I send him out West for the winter." He smiled sadly. "So that really does leave just me, unless you count Rosey."

"Not," said Darcy, "if there's another unsolved crime." She stood up and pulled a piece of paper out of her back pocket. "I drew up a sort of a contract," she said. "See what you think."

Brian unfolded the paper and read:

We the undersigned, being of sound mind and body, after our success in the Mystery of the Night Raiders, hereby swear to keep open minds in the face of all unexplained and unsolved crimes, believing that, as has been proved by the above case, there are ancient and monstrous creatures still in the world, capable of inflicting harm and imparting terror. And we further pledge that, as Monster Hunters, we will track down all such beings that come to our attention, and see that Justice is done.

"Whew!" said Numbles. "You must've used a dictionary for that one. Or a thesaurus."

"Both," said Darcy. "I even missed the beginning of our end-of-season team party yesterday, working on it. Well?"

"Holmes would laugh," said Brian, "but maybe he didn't know everything—even though his methods were perfect, of course. Sure, I'll sign."

He did and then passed the sheet to Numbles, who said "Why not?" and reached for a pen.

Darcy added her signature, and they joined hands three ways.

"Till the next monster," said Darcy solemnly, and Brian and Numbles echoed her words.